ON THE VERGE OF
SUICIDE

Presence of happiness is felt in its absence

Jack Stewart

ISBN
978-1-95737-816-9 (Paperback)
978-1-95737-815-2 (eBook)

"Description begins in the writer's imagination, but should finish in the reader's."

—Stephen King

TABLE OF CONTENTS

Author's Note... vii

Prologue... ix

Plan To Go To Another City... 1

The Day Of Departure 5

Experience Of The Journey...11

First Day In The Hostel 15

My Best Friend..19

Meeting With Katie Rose... 23

Katie Comes Closer.. 33

Mentally Disabled 39

Katie Proposes Me.. 45

Master Cyrus And Mrs. Katie 55

On The Verge Of Suicide.. 91

Epilogue.. 105

Upcoming Novel... 109

Author's Note

Whenever I read the news about people ending their lives, it upsets me to the core and others too who go through the same news must have felt the same.

I always wanted to prevent people from killing themselves but I am incapable of reading the minds and solving problems of each of them which is certainly not possible. Hence I decided to voice my message to general public through my work, since I too had faced the situation where life stops holding any value and gives us all possible reasons to finish it. At such situation, neither mind nor heart seems to be supporting us and we try to find comfort and solace in the arms of death. So I am quite aware of how to cross such hurdles in life and can tell you while doing so how it feels and how unbearable life becomes.

PROLOGUE

"Sir, the tap is closed. You need not worry about it". I said.

A person in black suit turned his head to look at me. He was about eighteen or nineteen years old. Black eyes, jet black hair and his white-shining face gave him an artificial look. 'Beautiful' is the word that can be used for him.

"Sorry sir, you were looking at it since past ten minute so I wanted to help you", I explained him, for his puzzled look.

"It's okay", he replied and smiled at me which was a sheer indication of his soft and gentle nature. It increased his beauty. Anyone would have been amazed at his charm. It was really difficult for me to distract my mind and eyes away from him. I wanted to keep looking at him as if I had been bewitched but then somehow I gathered myself up and thankfully got conscious of my stupidity and took my eyes off of him.

"Sir, if you don't mind, can you tell me why were you looking at the tap for so long?" I asked gathering the courage.

"There's a long story behind it", he retorted. It seemed as if he wanted to share some painful experience with me.

I became curious. And, I think, he noticed that curiosity in me so, after a while, he couldn't remain quiet anymore and went ahead, "Come, sit here. I'll tell you about this".

We sat together and he led off a conversation which can almost be termed as a monologue.

Plan To Go To Another City

I DON'T KNOW why I started loving her or how I started developing a strange feeling for her. I don't know whether she was the reason behind my success or she was responsible for the saddest phase of my life.

Sometimes, when you get a girl after many hardships, pain and especially sacrifice, then you may not have that much love for her. When she wants over-attention from you or when you are always the beginner of the conversation, then the relationship degrades. You should not always hide your feelings and love. Sometimes, it is necessary to express your love. It refreshes the relationship.

Perhaps, I also had the same experience related to this.

I was still in the secondary education group while my neighbourhood children had passed the whole of it. 'Pass' was, in fact, the word to which my teachers were allergic. They had bored my mind with the word 'toppers'.

For people, toppers are special human beings. They are alloys which is a mixture of gold, silver, platinum, diamond, pearl and a little bit of soil too.

I was a topper too but I had never allowed success to get into my head. I used to talk to everyone with a smile. This behaviour of mine was also taken as an advantage by others to misbehave with me.

Usually, a successful student keeps other students at an arm distance. He talks only to his fellow toppers. When he talks to failures he tries to talk to them in their style to show that there is a part of casual nature in him too.

Carol was not a topper. Carol is the name of the girl about whom I am talking.

Carol's full name was Carol Agresta and mine was Cyrus Cilestino. There was another girl. Her name was Katie Rose. She was just the opposite of Carol. She hardly called me Cyrus. 'Cyril' and 'Casper' were her habitual words but 'Cyril' was her favourite.

You can say that what Cyrus was to Carol, the same was Katie to Cyrus, or even more. I used to shower a lot of love on Carol. All the sacrifices made for that girl is worth writing in the form of books. But the love which Katie gave me was many times more than that I gave to Carol. I think Carol never expressed her love which was one of the major reasons of my sadness.

Students nowadays are very smart but students at that time were not that much. I followed my friends who were constantly updated with the whole students of Italy.

I wanted to become an engineer. I didn't want to become doctor because then I would always want the people to fall ill so that I could become rich.

Whenever you ask any greedy person that why he wants to become doctor, he will reply, "I want to serve the people". Actually, he is saying in his mind, "I want the people to serve me". For this greedy fellow, a good doctor is not the person who treats the patients well but a person who earns money well. 'Well' is not the correct word. Instead we should use the word 'rapidly'. So rapidly that even the growth of bacteria bows its head in front of this word 'rapidly'.

I had no friends but I'm still referring the persons close to me as 'friends'. Actually, they were so-called friends.

I expressed my desire of becoming an engineer to my friends. One of my friends introduced me to his senior. That senior fellow was an unauthorized career counsellor. He had been helping students like me for several years. Nobody knew or nobody had even dared to calculate how many students went through his advice.

"Hello!" I said. He shook his head with a smile.

He was really a senior, a comical senior and reserved type person. Actually he was senior in his thought.

Throughout his academic career, he had done a lot of researches and analysis. His researches comprised of various bitter truths of life—How a teacher teaches, how a teacher should teach, which books a teacher should refer, whether a teacher is teaching fast or slow, which coaching classes should a student go, how to pass board exams in one night, which teacher spoils the students, which students spoil the teacher, how to fight for your fundamental rights and so on.

His theories and researches were so abundant that different volumes of books could be created from it.

In spite of having all this greatness and great knowledge, he never excelled in academics because he never studied. It's as simple as that. Ultimately, you will be a failure in every field of studies by following his advice because your entire day will be wasted in remember his advice. Since he was the creator of all these principles, he had to waste his entire career. Instead of studying with planning, he used to spend his whole time researching on how to study and what to study. When he finished his planning, unfortunately, there was no time left for executing his plan.

Struggle had become the motto of his life as though he had gifted himself with the habit of struggle.

In spite of many failure attempts and frustrations, he was humble and modest in his behaviour to others. Though he was very rich, he treated his each friend with respect and tolerance which everybody appreciated.

Later I came to know that his efforts didn't go in vain and he became a very successful businessman.

"Want to become an engineer?", the senior asked me after hearing my whole story.

"No, an architect", I said in my mind. Was my whole speech not enough to acquaint him with my ambition for the profession of engineering?

"Yes", I replied.

"Work hard and be innovative. It's an excellent field for the innovative people", he advised.

"Is that all you have got to tell me?", I thought in my mind.

"If you face any trouble, you can call me for help. Don't hesitate and remain focussed on what you want to achieve", he said politely.

My friend, Alfredo Costanzo, then decided to take admission in Emerson College in Boston. And it was definite that I'd be admitted in one of the best schools in that city. I used to study higher classes material, though I was too young for that, due to my impatience for getting admission in MIT. We began searching for any cheap coaching classes that would prove useful in cracking MIT and Harvard entrance examinations. We could not afford to see our dreams crushing down at any cost. I sometimes lost focus on my studies but Alfredo was unperturbed by any distraction as if nothing could overwhelm him and stir him up. He was mature enough to survive even in a complete strange environment. We were clueless about the things we were going to face in a strange country, U.S., but we had relied upon each other.

The Day of Departure

I T WAS THE 5th of November. My friend Alfredo and I were prepared for leaving Milan.

Alfredo had got admission in one of the cheapest universities of Boston. And, I could not figure out the motive behind his decision. We could easily go for the best university as we were financially quite strong. But at the same it was obvious that to ask him the reason was not easy for me.

I centred around two things—my studies and Carol.

Finally the day arrived for which I had been waiting for so long. At the gate, we bid goodbye and went out for our destination. It was an emotional departure.

We hired a taxi which took us to the airport. Airport was near Carol's house. In fact, she was living in an airport colony. In school days, we frequently heard from Carol that she lived in an airport colony.

Everything seemed gloomy and the feeling of dejection had caused much distress to me. I thought of ending my life a million times, perhaps due to my incessant loneliness. My love for Carol kept me alive somehow. I thought Carol had feelings for me but sadly she never expressed. It had been quite long that I did not secure first rank. I was out of luck since 5 to 6 years. I thought life would go on like this and will never improve. One day, I will be left alone in a corner by all, including Carol for sure. The emptiness I was struggling against was killing me bit by bit each day. I might not have decided to commit suicide but the desire to lead my life any further had certainly got vanished.

When a person has lost interest in life and has decided to commit suicide, he can be called dead from that moment. Ending the life by killing himself is a mere formality. He can be called a dead body roaming to and fro without any aim.

When I met the senior, I was motivated a little and got encouraged by his attitude in dealing with failure. In spite of the innumerable discouragements received from life he never let himself be defeated completely and continued to fight against all odds and adversities and still managed to look happy with a great zeal. He set the first example of headstrong determination for me.

Alfredo and I were sitting idle with nothing to do. We had reached too early. Since Carol's house was located just at a walking distance from the airport, I was expecting Carol to come at nearby park taking the evening walk. Even a glimpse of her would have made my day. I could have slept a sweet sleep. A talk with her would have worked for me like an energy drink. A warm embrace would have taken off all my mental pressure and physical pain but touching before the marriage was against my moral instinct.

You always feel the need of the presence of someone in your life which would fill each day of your life with happiness. A person whom if seen in sadness can take away all your troubles and her smile helps to exude an extreme sense of happiness. The person is surely a female. She would come to the gate to kiss you goodbye accompanied by a hug when you go for a long journey. A kiss on the lips is the token of love which indicates your romantic mood and assurance of unconditional love for each other on returning. If it is on forehead, it symbolizes the purity of your love and a vow to protect her from all evils and also shows that you are very clean and have no desire. If it is on cheek, it signifies that you are a vegetarian lover. If it's on the neck, it tells about your uncontrollable emotions and shows that you were just on the edge of becoming excited. But these things may be believed for husband and wife only.

Even after a long wait, Carol was not seen. I became hopeless. All the romance with her was possible in my fantasy world only. However, in reality also, if she would have asked me to hook up with her I would have never agreed. I would not have even touched her and would wait till our marriage.

The time of the flight had still not come but I was not agitated by that. Instead, I was enjoying every bit of my time at the airport because it was adjacent to Carol's house.

This is what happens when somebody falls in love deeply. You like him whatever he does and how he does. You fall in love with his habits too and start following his each moves – you love how he eats, walks and even talks. Even the things which he uses become very dear to you no matter how invaluable it is. If he does not speak to you, you blame yourself and try to fix the matter anyhow but if any other person stops speaking to you, then you simply accuse him for this but not yourself.

The person whom you love plays a very important role in your life becoming a major part of it. You like to see him all the time. When you both are having a good conversation, you don't want to stop and want to continue it without caring about the time. In fact, he is the one who if comes to you when you are just about to kill yourself, you will go back to your normal life and start working hard enthusiastically to improve it. I had the same depth of love for Carol. She had curly hairs. There was another girl named Eloisa who studied with us. She had straight blonde hair. She was very popular for her beauty in school. But I always had been the ardent admirer of Carol. Her beautiful curly hairs used to mesmerize me. On the contrary, I didn't really appreciate Eloisa's straight hair who looked more like a British woman with hazy white complexion to me, though her blonde hair added to her beauty. Carol was totally different from her. Her face was spotless and had an appealing texture of glowing skin. She had a creamy complexion very similar to orange or transparent white. She had a pair of two twinkling jet black eyes and above all a calm posture. There was something different in her which singled her out from the crowd. She was not the type of girl who would start crying at the rebuke of a teacher. The politeness in her voice was capable of turning even the harsh words into a soft statement; it looked like she can't scold anybody. She would maintain her calmness even in her anger. She never shouted like other girls and always had control over her emotions. Eloisa, on other hand, lacked all these qualities. She never cried at little things. Her anger was worth watching. All these traits of hers made her look ugly to me. I wondered why all the students craved for her attention rather it seemed strange to me that none except me had ever fallen for Carol so deep and nobody even talked about her in school.

Perhaps, the reason behind this is not the person you look at but how you look at.

For me, behaviour and conduct are far more attractive in a person than the beautiful features. Hence, a rude-beautiful girl is of no value.

The world judges a person by his deeds and sense of morality. In fact, it's your character and success which add to your beauty. Your efforts may bring you success but it takes character to hold it.

I was ready to defend Carol in any kind of circumstances. If she wore fashionable clothes, I used to say, "Children should look smart and fashionable. They should wear such clothes as this is the right time to live your life fully and showcase your talents. Once the time is gone, it will never return". If she wore simple clothes, I used to say, "We should be simple and have high thinking. Carol sets an excellent example of this". If she brought plastic stationary box in school, I used to say, "Plastic boxes are safe to use. See, metallic box can get rusted, and if you get cut on your finger accidentally by it, the wound can get septic. Carol is well aware of all these advantages. She is really a smart girl". If she brought metallic box, I used to say, "Metallic boxes last long. They don't break easily. Beautiful designs on plastic boxes are pleasure to eyes but they do not last long and breaks sooner. Carol's preference is worth appreciating". Whenever she brought fruits in her lunch box, I used to say, "Fruits are the best source of all sorts of nutrition and your hands also don't get oily while eating". If she brought vegetables, I used to say, "This type of food is rich in energy. Though we all bring vegetables but the food Carol brings seems most nutritious. Moreover, we should not bring fruits in school". I admired and appreciated her choice in every way possible.

We were still at the airport waiting. I was enjoying the chilled weather outside to its fullest though I shivered some times. However, I was near Carol's house so it felt as if Carol, in the form of cool air, was blowing around me and touching me softly. I was thinking about Carol's apartment. For me, it was not only the house but the most beautiful palace of the world . . . most comfortable . . . most pleasing and the happiest one. Even the airport held a special attachment to me and became the best airport in the world. Everyone and everything related to Carol was special for me. But I was still waiting for the last glimpse of her before I left for Boston. It would have fulfilled my last wish. Certainly enough, I myself was unaware about the depth and sincerity of my love for her.

In the airport, there was a stall of magazine which had a large collection of vulgar magazines. It always annoys me to acknowledge that this type of stalls attract most customers. Perhaps, those customers are either very bold or too insensitive regarding the etiquette, social conduct and mannerism. I was informed by some of my friends that people visit these stalls with their faces covered with cloth, and after quickly buying these obscene magazines, they swiftly disappear. They sometimes allow the shopkeeper to keep the change, and in case of extra money accidentally given to the shopkeeper, they don't even consider taking the money back and hastily leave the stall so that nobody can recognize them. The shopkeeper also co-operates with his customers fully and do not smile throughout the deal. Finally, after a long wait, the time to depart arrived.

EXPERIENCE OF THE JOURNEY

IT WAS A comforting night. The scene outside was pleasant to behold. We were about to board the plane.

A few minutes before the boarding, the mobile rang. It was from home. Alfredo informed his mother that we were about to board the plane. He told her that I was suffering from acute headache. I started mocking myself that why I told Alfredo about my headache. The moment was draining me emotionally. The headache was due to inadequate sleep and not because of any tension or emotional departing. Everyone said that Cyrus's attachment and affection towards his home is intense. I was being consoled that – "You need not worry, Cyrus. We're there with you. It's not the matter of whole life. Moreover, we'll be in constant touch with you through internet". Now, the whole drama was becoming unbearable for me. I snapped quickly that I was not missing them but they were adamant on what they believed and instead told me that it was of no use to hide my love for them.

Alfredo fell asleep quickly as he was very tired. I was sitting on my birth recalling my memories with Carol and wished that she too would come along with me to Boston and study with me there.

Sometimes I used to think that perhaps the similarity we share in our names has sowed the seed of love within me for her.

Next I remembered the magazine stall. It brought smile on my face. There was a person standing near the stall having his eyes fixed on the hot magazines. I was constantly looking at him. When he finished his eye work, he looked at me. He understood that I caught him. After that, he always avoided eye contact with me. He didn't even look at any girl passing by. But he had already lost his prestige in my eyes, so there was no use of not looking at the girls.

There are some people who take off their eyes from the girls passing by and start looking at different directions. Even decent men would do the same but they soon realize their mistake. The perverts want to show that they are clean, but in reality, they take the opposite route usually. If they are wearing black sunglasses, they will just scan the girl. If they get the opportunity of sitting on the window side beside a girl, they will stick to the window side and start gazing outside but will never spare a single chance when the brake is applied or when the bus is turned right or left. But sadly enough, this theory is not applicable in case of good men.

I next remembered about the shopkeeper of the magazine stall who looked a bit different. He was not looking at any magazine. I thought he might be a man of strong character. But, as you know, it's not easy to prevent yourself from the distraction of such alluring stimuli. He might have already been satisfied while arranging them on the stall as he was looking lethargic in his movements. With the passage of time, my excitement got increased. I was waiting for Boston airport. Some of the passengers were going to Boston for their higher education like us but I was not interested in having conversation with them.

There was a guy sitting beside me. I was forced to talk to him because he had left no stones unturned for it. He asked few things about me. In the meantime, he mixed the facts of love which was my Achilles Heel. In no time, we became virtual friends and exchanged our mobile numbers to remain connected. But it was too early for me to turn a virtual friendship into a real one.

I was not the type of person who would discuss about the private matters of life with strangers. Some people say, "Tell me about your problems. Share it with me. Do not hesitate. Do you think I'll disclose it to anyone? I swear by my mother, I'll never do that". In fact, they are usually the ones who will unveil your secrets to everyone. Your problems will serve them as the spicy topic of gossip with their friends. 'Friends' is the wrong word here. Actually, they don't have any. They can betray anybody at any time in this world no matter it's you or their so-called friends. They are not trustworthy and reliable people. Whenever they meet their so-called friends, they express their exaggerated affection for them to the point of absurdity. It looks like they are the only people on earth who care for them which is obviously unreal. They will talk about the girls as if they have profound knowledge about them. My friends also talked about girls but they never crossed the line as severely as these people do. These people will often use this phrase – Do you know more than me about girls?

We were about to reach Boston in a few minute. I was still feeling lonely. I was thinking only about Carol. I had none in my life with whom I was too attached nor I had any close friend. I did not believe in sharing my problems with others anymore. I wanted to lead my life on my own terms but I was forced to live it in another way which was killing me from inside . . . . it was showing me the path of committing suicide. In fact, now I was a changed man, very different from what I used to be once.

Thankfully a little hope was still breathing into my heart which kept me alive; otherwise, it would have been a totally different story. My mind was being haunted by different thoughts – the people as they mock me now will continue after my death also saying that I was a loser who could not achieve anything in life and committed suicide. I will lose respect in everybody's eyes. Even my death can't solve my problem on the contrary it would be increased to the next level.

The plane landed on the Boston airport and from there we straight headed towards the hostel.

FIRST DAY IN THE HOSTEL

MY ROOM WAS booked one month prior. When I reached the hostel, its very first look created a good impression on me and I really liked it.

As soon as we entered the hostel, I saw many boys roaming here and there. Some of them looked immovable from their postures, sitting like a statue. These 'some of them' were the seniors who were still trying to crack the entrance exams. In course of time, they had witnessed so many suicides in their life that now the news of students committing suicide was no more the issue of concern to them. Such news did not shock them. They always had a fake smile on their faces which was very similar to their studies too. They never bothered about anything and there was no sign of tension on their faces. As it was a new experience for me, their callousness perplexed me to the core. A student has to fail many times to become such insensitive in nature. In comparison to them, I was a small bird recently hatched from an egg who was eager to learn how to fly.

We reached the reception sofa, where after sometime, an elderly person came to us. He was very courteous in his approach. I was instructed beforehand to wish him 'good morning' because I always used to forget that.

The elderly person greeted us with a smile.

"Good morning, sir!", he wished Alfredo first. Soon they finished, and it was my turn. I was speaking in a low voice. It was 6 to 7 hours passed that I did not have a single drop of water in my throat. My voice had lost its strength. It could not reach his ears. He nodded reading my lips. Sometimes, just nodding the head works for us. But Alfredo wanted to introduce us clearly so he was disappointed.

Nelson Baker, the elderly person, accompanied us to our room and also opened it for us. It was Room No. 5.

'5' was my lucky number but surprisingly enough it was chosen randomly by me without any reason.

Nelson handed over to us all the essential things and went away.

It was a pleasant morning. I took bath and began to arrange my things in the room. It was a spacious room beautifully decorated. It also had few beautiful things kept there. It had valuable stuffs kept for knowledge and educational purpose.

In the bathroom, while brushing teeth, I saw many romantic scripts written by romantic persons of romantic eras. There was a wonderful sticker stuck on the mirror which could help your morning become interesting and revitalizing. All these must have been done by the previous occupants of the room.

The stickers on bathroom mirror were really electrifying and arousing. I thought it was not right to indulge into these things and get distracted. I removed them all except one. It was different from the rest. I thought of replacing the facial part of the sticker with Carol's photograph. But again it would have hurt Carol's feelings and it was morally degrading too. So I declined the idea. But if I would have done it, I would have definitely got fainted inside the bathroom.

It was an air-cooled room where there was no fan so that a student couldn't hang himself and so neither could I. There was a roof of net all placed over the veranda. If you try committing suicide jumping from any floor of the hostel you will be caught in net and you'll be saved. Thus, the idea of committing suicide by jumping from the building gets struck off from the list. The owner of the hostel, Vivian Shepherd, according to me, had tried all means possible to prevent students from killing themselves. The students had no option left. Now the students could only wait for their death one day without anybody catching them doing so red handed.

The motto of Mr. Shepherd's arrangements was to let students understand that, instead of trying different ways to end their lives, it's better and much easier to put to use their talents in making efforts to live their lives happily.

While arranging things my eyes fell on a big note written on a bookshelf. It read – 'Life may not offer you the same opportunity many times. Make hay while the sun shines and always remember that you are not studying for your parents but for yourself'. This note was in capital letters perhaps to attract the attention as it was inspiring no doubt. But it worked as a surprise for me. I wondered how somebody can write on the bookshelf and that too using an ordinary pen. In addition to that, there was a similar note carved on the side of the same bookshelf saying, "Never take this room. You will ruin your life. Vivian Shepherd is . . . .". I got anxious reading the note and immediately informed Alfredo and showed him everything. He assured me that nothing bad was going to take place. Alfredo was, however, very much impressed with the last line of the big note as it featured something related to parents.

Room No. 3 was just in front of my room whereas Room No. 4 was adjacent to mine and Room No. 3. Room No. 4 shared the same washroom with mine. The washroom had two doors – one in my room and the other in Room No. 4. The entrance of Room No. 3, 4 and my room formed a square with its one side removed. Room No. 3 had two occupants and Room No. 4 had only one occupant. The occupants of both Room No. 3 and 4 were engineering students. The guy of Room No. 4 had his surname 'Carlos' and one of the two boys of Room No. 3 also had the same surname. A guy from Room No. 3 who was not a Carlos, left the hostel and took room somewhere else. There was another Carlos who was living on the third floor. Somehow he got to know about the vacancy and without wasting a minute, he decided to shift in Room No. 3 which means all my neighbours now were 'Carlos'.

As expected, in a few days, third floor's Carlos shifted to Room No. 3.

My Best Friend

THE 5TH AUGUST was the day we reached Boston. The classes were scheduled to commence from the 26th of November.

We arranged our belongings in place first. After a few hours, we were about to receive our lunch. Alfredo went to purchase all the necessary things we required but in a hurry forgot to take his wallet with him. I was expecting him to return soon. Few minute had passed where I heard the door being knocked. I thought it might be Alfredo. I was right but partially because he was accompanied by a family who had come from Venice. Actually they had come to see their son who was staying in Room No. 3. Alfredo introduced me to them. He too was introduced to me by his parents. His name was Simon. He was very polite and gentle. He was perfect to become an ally. He fitted well in my description of a friend. But, I thought, he deserves someone better than me as his friend. Because the cruelties of this mean world had transformed me into a bitter man and I considered every person as mean and selfish. Perhaps that was the reason Simon did not like me and we could not be the type of friends we could. I was impressed by his simplicity so much that at some times even Carol seemed to fade a little from my memory. He was always there to motivate me and talked with me with sheer positivity in his voice. We used to sit together for lunch and breakfast. Since the timing of our classes differed, we sometimes missed our meals together. During holidays and Sundays, we never missed our dinner together. Without exaggerating the fact, it was his presence in my life which helped me to realize that I was alive. Once again, my life seemed to be resurrected in me. He was not like other crooked people. He was lively person who used to joke and talk about different things apart from studies. We became so close to each other that whenever he went to his uncle's house on holiday, I started noticing his absence around. He was the one who spoke to me first. He was the one to wish me before anybody. He was the one who shared my problems. He was always afoot in friendship than me. I could never return the affection and sincerity he gave me. Perhaps I lacked warmth as a human being and had become super cold which hurt Simon a lot. He must have felt it in his heart but never tried to be vocal about it. I could read it on his face. Our friendship was deteriorating day by day. In order to repair his hurt feelings, he began to avoid me. His negligence did not cause me much trouble though he tried a lot as his soft nature was not that hurtful. He used to smile at me and moved his eyebrows as a sign that we both are not new to each other. He rarely spoke to me. At times, he threw tantrums on me to overcome his frustration. But I did not feel bad and thought his behaviour towards me was justified. The rude behaviour of someone you love disturbs your heart, mind and even soul. It's the wound beyond cure. The pain intensifies and becomes unbearable. If someone you care but not to the point of loving them madly hurts, the pain remains there but not at the cost of taking away peace from your mind. You do not expect anything from them in return.

Gradually the affection disappeared and it was no more a congenial friendship but an exceedingly burdensome acquaintance. No more personal talks, no more eating meals together, no more listening to each other's problems and greeting with love and affection – we had lost our connection completely. He ate lunch with another guy who was also an engineering student, and I ate with a guy who was my classmate in coaching classes. Occasionally if we ever get to eat in his company, he did not speak to us or actually me.

I was again in the trap of loneliness which overshadowed me. Once again, I tugged myself away from the world. I went back to my old self, the same mentally sick person carrying the load of life quietly and painfully. The recurring thoughts of suicide started to visit my mind redundantly. The enthusiasm of life was dead deep inside. In spite of all this, I never attempted to end my life but my heart always screamed for help to put an end to my sufferings. Often times I got drowned in my dark thoughts so deep that I would not even care if somebody would try to kill me rather I would be grateful to his generous act because the depression used to make me numb and had impaired my rationality totally. I wished if somebody could manage to kill me without my knowledge so that I would be relieved from the accusation of committing suicide. The sadness took me to the point of madness. I guess my subconscious mind always looked for the one important person who could kill me. He should attack me from back and not from the front because then I'll have to defend myself which could save me. Moreover, I wanted him to attack me so hard that I would die in one shot.

Days passed but I was not satisfied with what I had achieved till now. I was still struggling with my life.

I was in constant contact with my dear ones from home but even their love was unable to soak up my pain. Even they could not provide me the emotional support I needed. I was performing quite well in my academics but I needed to work harder to reach the top. Simon's study material proved very beneficial to me during our friendship days. Since he was a sincere and regular student, his study material was much advanced than mine. It helped me immensely while preparing. My loved ones were always concerned about me. They always asked me if I had any problem. Somewhere in my heart I was regretting for my behaviour towards Simon. I should have also tried to strengthen our bond. I felt guilty of breaking the beautiful bond we once shared. It was me who could never understand and value the importance of sacrifice in a relation so dear to us.

Victor Carlos, a guy newly shifted in Room No. 3, was standing in front of me at his door. I could see Simon through open door sitting on the bed. Coming out of my room, I shut the door and Victor too came forward to have a talk with me. As soon as we started our conversation, Simon stepped off the bed and closed the door without looking at me. I was deeply hurt. His ignorance stirred me emotionally. It was a heart-wrenching experience to see our bond crumbling away. For a moment I was lost in my own world and could not pay heed to Victor's questions. All my attention was concentrated on Simon and our weakening friendship. Victor asked for my study material. It sounded queer to me as he was Simon's roommate. I told him that my notes were not up to the standard but he remained implacable. I was already disturbed due to Simon's behaviour and now Victor's repeated demands were annoying me. At last I agreed to give him all my notes without losing my temper. I walked out of the alley of Room No. 3, 4 and 5. Suddenly Victor stopped me and asked, "What's your surname?". He did not wait for me to answer and promptly said, "Is your surname Carlos?". It was quite foolish but I restrained myself from uttering anything worse and simply replied, "Yes". Victor smiled in surprise. He said, "What a coincidence! All the students in this alley are Carlos. I am Carlos. My room partner is Carlos. A guy from Room No. 4 is Carlos too, and now see, you are also Carlos". All of a sudden, the door of Room No. 3 opened and Simon appeared. Victor, in excitement, conveyed the same message in the same manner to Simon. Simon nodded and hardly paid any heed to it. He walked past me without looking at me. This time, I was really hurt and broken inside. I was about to head towards the nearby park for a walk but I changed my mind and quietly slipped into my room and sat on a chair resting on my back. The whole experience I had was mournful. I was guilt-ridden. I was cursing myself and lastly I began weeping bitterly as a small child. I was unable to stop my tears from rolling down the cheeks. I knew that I had lost my best friend and now it was beyond repair.

Meeting With Katie Rose

ON THE 21ST day of November, I was very excited to attend an open session organised by Daniel Institute five days before the first class where we were made to swear to work hard and accomplish our goal of becoming a skilful engineer.

On the previous night of 20th November, the thoughts of what would happen the next morning in the open session kept me awake for the whole night.

In the morning, I was discussing with Alfredo about the events going to take place in the open session which was scheduled to be held in the evening.

There was a horrible surprise for me. In the afternoon, Alfredo informed me that a family from Ukraine had come to meet their son who is also an engineering aspirant. He too had joined Daniel Institute. We were supposed to attend the open session with them. At this very information, my heart sank as I despised anybody's company except Alfredo.

At 6:55 PM in the evening, we all departed towards the open session. We were running against the time due to that Ukrainian boy who took more than an hour to bath.

Within 5 minute the open session was going to start being scheduled at 7:00 PM. We had covered the distance from the hostel to the institute in 5 minute. Peter Hill, the Ukrainian boy, had a reserved nature though he belonged to a very jovial family. He never spoke a word except to few people around him. The arrival of this guy just added to my miserable life. I was already emotionally drowned for my recent ruined friendship with Simon, and now to bear the unfriendly and silent behaviour of that guy was like a punishment for me for breaking Simon's heart.

The saying, "What goes around comes back around", meaning your bad deeds are paid by your sufferings, was seeming true in my case.

Somehow we managed to reach the premises of Daniel Institute at 6:59 PM. Throughout the journey from hostel to Daniel Institute, Peter did not utter a single word. It was just when I asked him about his scores in different subjects during his schooldays, that he spoke. First I thought that Peter's surrounding is to be blamed for his distant behaviour. I thought that the surrounding is responsible for the moulding of behaviour of an individual but certainly it was not the case with Peter. Peter was naturally like that. Nobody provoked him to be like that.

Every man in this world exhibits their own way of dealing with life, in other words, all of us reveal different types of personality traits. Some are of gentle nature and are cool headed who do not allow their aggravating emotions to disrupt their calmness. Even though they are angry, they are able to suppress it and deal with the situation in a controlled manner; on the other hand, some are of impulsive nature and they can't withhold their anger and get burst which eventually cause them trouble. They cover up their mistakes by saying, "I can't control my anger. I am not in my senses when I'm angry and I say whatever comes to my mind though my intention is not to let down or hurt anyone". By the time they realise their mistakes, it's already too late to set it right, and all they can do is to repent for their reckless deeds. It was truly said by a philosopher that a man is hidden under his own tongue.

Daniel Institute was beautifully decorated with colourful ribbons and flowers. The entire staffs were present in the auditorium. Some senior faculties were busy managing the show on stage and some were helping them in order to run the show successfully as well as to provide the best service to the audience. It was giving more of an impression of a university. Many of the faculty members were eminent personalities. Mark Casper and Paul Philemon, the very famous teachers among all, were almost known to everybody for their inspirational and motivational stories of struggle in life.

It was a great pleasure to witness such inspiring figures in front of me. I had only seen them in pictures in the prospectus which I received while registering my name in the institute during my stay at Milan. When they occupied the stage, tears welled up in our eyes listening to their stories especially in the eyes of our parents as the story itself dealt with parents slightly. Perhaps it must have struck on some sensitive issues of their lives related to their own parents. Some of them might have lost them at a very tender age too. Every individual is emotionally attached to his parents no matter he's a kid or a grown up. A fully grown up person has the same love for his parents like that of a small child; it's just the level of maturity which sets them apart from each other. As the love matures, it becomes sensible; so though the affection for parents may not be outwardly perceived in a grown up man, it is no less than found in a kid. When we see a man sitting beside the corpse of his mother or father, he holds back his emotions and tries not to weep, and we take it as a sign of unfeelingness. Not only a child but an adult too cries, wants to have fun and roam about. Being a grown up person, he is supposed to be mentally strong and keep his emotions in check.

As the rest of the other spectators, I too was enjoying the open session. The other teachers also came forward to share their own story of hardships, and they all were surprisingly amazing. Moreover, we all were made acquainted with the history of Daniel Institute. It was a note-worthy experience.

During the open session, I met a girl, Katie Rose, who left an indelible footprint on my mind. In fact, the love she poured on me was unconditional and impossible to get faded.

I met her by coincidence. Actually I was sitting with Alfredo, Peter and Peter's family in one of the last rows of the auditorium. As soon as we reached, the auditorium seemed to be tightly packed. I was sitting on the left of Peter, whereas Alfredo was seated on his right. On Alfredo's right side, Peter's father was sitting while on the right side of Peter's father, Peter's mother was sitting. Our sitting arrangement gave me and Katie Rose to bind with each other. To my left side, there were two chairs unoccupied so I placed my bag on the last one. There was a man sitting on my left. He might be of twenty-one or twenty-two years old judging by his looks. He more looked like a freshly passed-out engineering student. To me, every person carrying such a heavy look was a graduate and that too an engineering one. Behind our row was the wall of the auditorium and also on the left side of the chair bearing my bag was the wall of the auditorium. We were on the edge of the rectangular auditorium.

The man sitting next to me looked like a native of U.S. I told Peter that the man might be from the United States itself or the Great Britain. Peter just smiled and nodded as per my expectations. I also did not expect anything more from him. But I was getting curious to know about the man with each passing minute, so finally breaking my silence, I asked him in his native language where he had come from. He looked at me and explained, "I am an American. I was born here. I was brought up here by my parents. They were also born here. The owners know my family well. My sister and I have come from New York to attend this open session because of our friendly relations". He spoke all this amidst my different other questions.

Next I asked him, "Has your sister gone?".

He replied, "No, she has gone to meet her friend, Suzy. Suzy is living under the guardianship of Paul. My father personally knows Paul and has requested him to look after Suzy. She is living in Daniel Institute's hostel only". We had a lucid conversation. Peter's parents and Alfredo were busy among themselves while Peter was busy in himself.

I think that the man was deliberately sitting on one of the last benches in order to avoid interaction with people or perhaps did not want to become the centre of attraction but we shared a good rapport. He also told me that his name was William Cook.

In the meantime, my eyes all of a sudden fell on a girl coming towards us. She was asking every student and parent sitting on that row to shift their legs and provide her space to move forward towards her seat. At the same time, she unwillingly became the centre of attraction which, I think, she disliked. Every parent took a sharp look at her but it was obvious when any charming person passes by. She had a different looks from the normal standard. I avoided her to mitigate her uneasiness. As she neared a chair, she noticed that the bags were kept on her chair. She, in her silent language, asked about the owner of those bags. Like a gentleman I picked them up. I thought she would sit on that chair. But to my utter surprise, she silently asked her elder loving brother to shift to the next chair. When she sat on the chair, it felt as though the chair was about to break. She was not fat but was well built, almost twice or thrice of my size, but shorter than me. I was slightly taller than her. She had brown hair that gave out exciting smell of her hair oil. Even her body perfume made the air around us pleasant. She looked very beautiful and her innocent face enhanced her beauty even more.

"She's my sister", William introduced her to me.

"Hi!", she said. I just smiled in shyness. Till then I looked very attractive . . . even to the boys. I was not kind of a person whom you could compliment with the words handsome and sexy. I looked more like a beautiful girl with dark black eyes and long eyelashes. The eyebrows appeared well shaped as though beautifully sketched by a pen. The jet black hairs (flaunting style) were always scattered over my forehead. I was very lean and thin like a girl. I did not have robust health rather was very weak. On the other hand, it looked as if whole of me could fit inside Katie's body easily as she had a study physique.

"He's Cyrus. He has come from Milan. He too is an engineering aspirant and has come to this city to study at Daniel Institute".

"That's nice", she showed her interest and continued, "We also had gone to Milan once. We visited many historical places there. It was such a great experience. I would love to go there again. I am very fond of the foods of that city". She then asked, "Which school did you study at, Cyrus?".

"German School of Milan, it's a historical school", I replied. I was impressed by her outspoken behaviour in the very first meeting. I never saw a girl being so candid with a stranger in the very first talk. She pronounced my name in a manner as though she knew me since long time. She was constantly gazing into my eyes. Unfortunately, I was not that smart to comprehend the real intentions behind those signals.

She retorted, "Yes, German School of Milan is a historical one" and smiled but I chose to remain non- reactive. She coaxed me to speak few words in German to which I politely obliged.

"Which school did you study at?" I asked her.

"Trinity School", she replied humbly. I got stunned at her reply. I had frequently searched about that school. It was one of the most expensive schools of U.S. She seemed to be quite interested in me which left me a bit disturbed. Then she furthered the conversation, "Where have you taken the room?".

"I am staying in a hostel", I replied.

"Which one?", she asked again. This question came as a surprise to me.

"Vivian Hostel....... Vivian Boys' Hostel. It's a boys' hostel", I emphasised a little.

Throughout the open session, we shared a lot of information about each other. She told me that she had finished her high school and is looking forward to pursue her study in a renowned university. Through our conversation, I figured out that she was quite good in her studies.

But later on I got to know that she was not only good in studies but extraordinary.

I couldn't concentrate on what was happening on stage and missed a few things of the open session. And I think, Katie's mind would not have gathered even that. Katie was out of her control and every now and then she seemed to switch over to the talk of romance. She was not missing any opportunity to touch me. Holding the cheeks like we do with a child, holding hands and other activities of her were a clear indication of her amorous advances towards me. Had we been alone there, she would have dragged me into a room and would have squeezed and exhausted me. Her brother seemed to be indifferent to all these and didn't really showed any sign of denial. Moreover, I think he himself was in favour of it. But to all these I got frightened.

"Cyrus, do you have any girlfriend?", Katie inquired. I understood that she had finally decided to gamble with her luck. But I was hesitating to answer anything.

I stuttered, "I . . . . I ".

She annoyed, "What I . . . .? Tell me, Cyrus, do you have any? . . . . Cyrus, I had never been so much attracted to any boy in my life . . . . you are the only one whom I am talking to so romantically you are the only person with whom I have fallen in love . . . . and that too so quickly and so deeply. I am getting crazy, Cyrus".

"I I don't have any but you can be called one and the first", I replied.

"Really!", she exclaimed in over-excitement and started blushing. I think her brother also knew that I was the one and only whom she got attracted to so he too didn't protest.

Katie's inquiry about my love interest had already revealed as well as removed all my doubts regarding her love for me.

Katie had totally lost her control. She was all set to make any sort of physical contact with me. She was at the verge of her wish fulfilment as soon as the lights went off. Out of nowhere we were informed by someone in the dark that there was a short circuit. After a few minute, the news spread through the workers that power backup solutions were unable to fix the problem. The wind began to blow gently giving the sensation of shivering cold. In the presence of our parents, an aura of calmness pervaded throughout the auditorium even at such situation. All the students were silent and waiting for the lights. Had there been no parents, the auditorium would have exploded with their noise creating a huge pandemonium.

Everyone was enjoying the cool air and drizzling rain. My body started shivering, teeth doing their job sincerely, as I was very weak. Suddenly, I was encircled by a heavy arm. I heard Katie saying, "Cyrus, don't refuse". As the lights were yet to come, she didn't want the opportunity to slip from her hand, and she advanced towards me. There was enough time for her to satiate her desire.

I felt as if even the nature was in favour of her, and both nature and her fate collaboratively intrigued against me weaving her destiny as she yearned. No doubt she experienced the serendipity. The lights went off just when she was going through bouts of arousal. In addition, it started raining. The breeze started blowing and touching our skin gently. She had a trembling sheep with fear sitting beside her. The lion, Katie, was about to pounce upon it. When the lights were there, she left no opportunity to touch me without caring much about the people around. I was fearful had she even lost that much of senses in herself, she would have made me sit in her lap and wetted me with her kisses.

It can be interpreted in the other way round that the lights were sure to go off, the rain was sure to start, and the cool air was sure to blow, and all these helped Katie to plot her mischievous activities against me in dark.

"Please leave. Please, don't do this. It's not right", I pleaded as I struggled with my full strength to get out of her grip. She again tried to take me into her arms. Now, I got confirmed that I took the wrong seat. Except the two of us, everyone was busy looking at the attempts of the workers to arrange things in order. Anyone at her place would have hesitated to do so but Katie had lost all her morality and had become shameless. If she would have applied a bit more force to hold me, I would have almost suffocated to death. She wanted to fulfil her desires at any cost. And, I too was audacious to destroy her intentions at any cost. During that scuffle, she even tried to pull me towards her but then I gave such an angry look that she completely withdrew her efforts. I was shivering with cold and above that her stupid amorous attempt was taking my suffering to the next level.

After some time, to my rescue, the lights came back. I covered my face with the fingers in sadness. I could not make noise too because then the matter could have become worse.

Katie had disappointed me. I had never even touched a girl neither had gazed any girl. Even If my eyes fell on any girl by coincident, I used to take them off of her.

If your eyes meet up with any girl by mistake, you should take them off her and shouldn't gaze any further. If you succeed in continuing the same pattern of behaviour and maintain it throughout your life, you will surely get a girl as your life partner who will be beautiful beyond your imagination.

Katie had gone against my ethical views. She had committed a sinful act in my opinion. She might not have been aware about that but I knew she had done wrong. She had broken my heart as well as lost her dignity in my eyes.

"Sorry, Cyrus! Please forgive me. I could not control myself . . . . I I'm extremely sorry. For God's sake, forgive me", Katie begged for forgiveness. I was annoyed by her behaviour and chose not to pay attention to her. I just kept my face covered with my hands and remain silent. She continued to speak.

"You should not have done this. It is not good morally. We should not forget our limits before marriage", I said. I did not mean to marry her. I just said the word 'marriage' with respect to all the young people out there but she took it as our marriage. She smiled and looked bashful.

My silence was unbearable for her, so she pestered, "Cyrus, speak to me. I won't repeat again. I promise to keep our relationship clean till our marriage". I was speechless. I mean, we were there to attend the open session, and she was talking about marriage. I couldn't make out why I had to face such awkward situation in life. It was too much for me to handle.

I reciprocated firmly, "I am a newcomer here. I want to qualify the entrance exams at any cost. I have no idea of how to strategise my study to score better. If I'll indulge myself in these activities, I'll not be able to achieve my dreams . . . . I am scared and under a lot of pressure right now". Her complacent smile confused me. She was actually smiling at my childlike behaviour of fearing the exams. "Don't worry about that. I'll help you in qualifying that", she tried to comfort me. I was relieved a bit. Her words genuinely put me at ease. Her offer of help lessened my trouble a bit.

"Will you help me qualify MIT entrance too?", I asked curiously. "Yes, my cute child, MIT too. We will make our after marriage destination in

MIT!", she replied casually and smiled. She was planning to marry me as soon as possible.

"Today is one of the most memorable days of my life", she exclaimed in delight.

"Mine too". I replied. Hers was in terms of love while mine was in terms of my dreams, in other words, qualifying MIT entrance exams.

The open session had ended. We both exchanged our contact numbers and bade each other goodbye and went to different directions.

Katie Comes Closer

I T WAS THE 25th of November. I was alone in my room at night. So I went out to take a short walk. I stood in the veranda and gazed at the moon and the stars.

The breeze was blowing hard making my hairs scattered on my forehead. The pleasant atmosphere of the night was soothing for me physically as well as mentally which I really needed at that point of my life.

After some time, I returned to my room. I remembered that once the warden had told me that after a few days, I'll get used to live alone.

Simon had gone out of his room to fill his jug with water but did not close the door. At that time, Simon was my friend and Smith Reese was his room partner. Victor had not yet shifted. Smith was a bit slothful in appearance but was good in studies.

While returning after filling the bottle, Simon met me in the way.

"Has Alfredo gone?", asked Simon in a usual sweet and polite voice.

"Yes", I replied.

"Come to our room. Let's have some talk", Simon suggested.

"No, I want to sleep. I'm very excited about my first class. I'm very tired too. Tomorrow we'll meet", I replied.

"It's okay", Simon replied. "But tomorrow, we'll meet after returning from the institute. I want you to tell me about your first class and also show me your booklets", he continued.

"Yes", I affirmed.

I entered my room. As soon as I picked up my mobile, I found several missed calls from Katie. I called her back but it got disconnected after a few rings. As per my expectations, she called me back after some time and we had a long conversation. She extended the talk whenever I wanted to hang up the call. She finally understood my discomfort and ended the conversation saying, "We'll meet tomorrow. Love you, Cyril. Goodnight and sweet dreams".

For the first time in my life, someone had spoken to me so politely. No matter how tough you appear outwardly, you naturally melt inside when someone offers you such sweetness in their talk.

Parents say that when a girl speaks so politely to their son, automatically he surrenders himself to her. There is nothing unusual in it. When a person speaks to you so sweetly, you will certainly start loving that person. But if those parents have a daughter, they want every man, whom they approach, to fall in love with their daughter. There should be a line of men to ask for her hand. Their son-in-law should become a true devotee of their daughter. She should rule his house and he should forget his own parents. These kinds of events usually happen.

Katie's talk on the phone would usually be like – 'At last, happiness has come into my life. I have become more lively now. I have become more protective about myself. I don't even want to sleep so that I can utilise that time too to think about you and the time we spent together. This is so special for me.'

I think Katie had come in my life in place of Simon with whom my friendship was going to face the test of the time in the near future.

The next morning, Katie came to meet me in my room. Her family members had convinced the owner of the hostel to come to my room. Since my room as well as my neighbours', Room No. 3 and Room No. 4, were usually silent, they did not have any problem. It was never crowded and mostly nobody passed by it. Katie knocked the door in a different style which later became her trademark way. Her way of knocking was very different from that of the others. It really was. She was dressed in blue sweatshirt and black cotton jeans and looked perfect, neither too tight nor too loose. Actually, any person wearing outfit of such colour combination could attract me easily, and if that person is Katie then it is worth seeing.

As she entered, I quickly closed the door which was the first thing I did whenever she came into my room. She did not sit on chair or bed but was standing at a corner of the room leaning against the wall. She was feeling guilty for her mistake committed the last night.

"How are you, Cyrus?", she started the conversation. "I am fine. I was hoping that you'll come", I said.

"Come, sit on the bed", I continued. She was overjoyed at this and took it as a sign of my forgiveness. She came forward to hug me. Now, again she was going to commit another mistake. It would have really been a bone-breaking experience for me. Moreover, I think, it would not have been her fault. Her physique was such that whether she would have held my biceps or pulled my cheek or whether she would have hugged me, it would have been fatal.

"I was really missing you, Cyril. For the whole night I could not sleep properly", she said stepping away from me. Although her embrace would have been a great pleasure, and her body odour and perfume was alluring, but I did not want to violate my moral beliefs. I politely signalled her to maintain distance.

If she would have embraced me, I would have felt charged with high-voltage current. Leave the thoracic contact, some shameless people make an abdominal one while hugging a girl. But anyhow, had it been the abdominal in my case, I would have inseminated as neither I was too energetic nor too powerful to suppress such hormonal activity.

Katie made another effort to come closer but this time I didn't mind and I would have never minded it, because she had promised me to help me in cracking the MIT entrance exams. So I had already started loving her. When you love someone truly, you will never mind any of his activities. You will anyhow try to bring out good qualities of that person, and definitely Katie had created such a place in my heart for herself.

Katie moved forward and fell on the bed. It was a very large double bed set which gave her more space to stretch herself. How can I forget such a jaw-dropping moment seeing her stretching on a huge bed! Even a professional wrestler would have put his guard down and refused to fight her. The whole bed was almost covered by her. Her stretched legs were tucked on each other and the hands in a crossed position were placed at the back of her head. She stretched to her fullest. Eventually her shirt was about to move up a little which was a bit embarrassing for me. Though nothing was visible still I preferred to be on the safer side and looked away.

"Your bed is very comfortable. It's cosy. How good is your room! Everything here is excellent. It's a pleasure to be here. I feel like staying here forever. How lucky you are, Cyril!", she said with her eyes closed.

She almost liked each and everything of mine. In fact, she loved my room . . . . my bed.......... and everything connected to me. But I think she was too young to understand the psyche of a person in love. Perhaps she was not aware of the fact that if I would have been living in her home and she, in mine, then also she would have felt the same way and would have yearned to stay at my place. It was not the matter of liking but matter of heart itself.

She was talking incessantly and her voice was becoming more and more sleepy. She looked at me. "What happened, Cyril? You are looking there", she said as she noticed that I was sitting with my eyes looking towards the other direction.

"No. Nothing . . . . I I was just thinking about my studies", I stammered a little.

"Oh! Don't worry about that. I'll handle that. You just enjoy and take care of your health", she consoled. "Cyril, I think, you are very weak. You are not even my half", she further spoke in a sleepy tone. She started lecturing me on my health. I don't know what she said afterwards because her voice was fading away gradually. Soon, she fell asleep.

Now I could feel her love for me when I realized that she was missing me so much that she could not sleep properly at night. Her sleepy eyes, tired body and quickly falling asleep were acting as an evidence of the fact that she really had feelings for me. While sleeping she looked innocent . . . . even more than when she was awake. Apart from me, any guy would have kissed her at that time but I was determined to have control on my nerves.

She was sleeping as a small child who has no tension in his mind except of playing. But, I think she had one tension in her mind all the time. And, it was of achieving my love.

Her shirt was still not placed in the most appropriate manner. I could no longer bear it as a silent observer and went by her side. I tried to pull down her shirt. But, I couldn't even move her, forget about lifting her and pulling down the back part of her shirt. She suddenly woke up. I was surprised to know that her sleep was so light. She smiled at me. She was glad to see me by her side.

"I was pulling down your shirt. It had gone up a little while you stretched. I thought it was not right, so I tried to bring back to its position . . . . Sorry to disturb your sleep", I explained her. But she was not interested in my explanations because she didn't want me to think that she was suspicious about me or doubted my character.

She wanted to show that she trusted me completely.

And, I feel, in reality also, she did.

"You were worried about this . . . . Boys take advantage of girls . . . . You're still a small child, Cyril", she said with her eyes half closed and lips smiling with joy. "It was a very sweet sleep. Till now, I have never slept such a sleep. It would have been sweeter if you . . . . Leave it. Come on, Cyril, let's have breakfast together But, I think you might have had it. You are also an early riser. Isn't that true?".

I replied, "No, I haven't eaten yet".

"That's good! Let's have it together", she exclaimed joyfully. She took her mobile and ordered breakfast in a serious tone. I had never seen this side of her. Though for others it was polite and not serious but for me it was strange as I had never seen her to be serious because she, while talking to me, looked as if she had forgotten everything and was completely lost into me.

After finishing the call, Katie said that the breakfast was on its way. Till the breakfast arrived, we talked to each other. Since it was morning and the environment too was quite romantic, our sweet talks made it perfect.

Our environment predominantly affects our moods. We generally talk, behave and react according to our mood. If it is day time and there is sweat-trickling heat, then we don't feel romantic . . . . We don't feel any lust. We can't enjoy movie with the sun shining over our head. If it is the night and we are amidst the cool air blowing, everything feels good and pleasant to us. You will never think about proposing your girlfriend on a burning desert where both of you are dead tired and thirsty where neither you are in a position to propose nor she is in a position to be proposed. If any person, in our locality or in our family, expires, we remember his funeral along with the weather of the day. If the dogs were barking outside your house at that time, then the memory of that day gets imprinted on your mind as a fearful moment of your life. If you are enjoying with your friends and suddenly the news of your neighbour's death comes to you, it will be imprinted on your mind in the a different way than the usual.

After about half an hour, Katie's servant brought our breakfast who arrived in a super-luxurious car.

Though Katie was never vocal about her richness, but if you have power, it will be expressed one day in any form.

"Today, you will eat with me only. Leave your hostel breakfast", Katie said as she began to open the packet.

"What does your father do?", I asked.

"He's a businessman", Katie replied and continued further, "Come on Cyril. Let's start and finish it".

"No, I can't eat this much. I don't have such a big appetite", I said.

"What No! You have to eat it. See your health. I don't want to say this but . . . . see, your body looks like a hanger. It looks as if clothes are hung on the hanger . . . you should take care of your health. Take it seriously, Cyril. It can affect your studies. Maybe you are not serious regarding your health but I am . . . . you . . . . you're . . . . you're my life, Cyril. You . . . . please Cyril, eat it for my sake", Katie almost scolded.

Katie was very possessive for me just like I was for Carol. If I could replace Carol with Katie, each day of my life would have been heavenly. Katie was so caring and concerned about me that she decided to plan a daily complete diet chart of breakfast for me. After a few days, lunch, snacks and dinner were also added to it. That day, I had to eat the breakfast to my fullest which made me feel like dying due to over- eating.

Mentally Disabled

I HAD OVER-EATEN that morning. Actually, I had taken my breakfast in perfect quantity according to the diet prescribed for the boys of my age. I was suffering with the loss of appetite; consequently I used to eat very less. So when Katie insisted me to eat, it seemed too much for me.

After eating so much, I was unable to even move. I lied down on my bed. I was sleepy. Till now, I was having a great time and the thought of suicide had completely vanished from my mind. There was now only one problem left to me, which was about Carol.

I couldn't figure out why I was still dissatisfied. But I guess, it's not only with me. It's the problem of every living human being on earth. There is always a new drama waiting for us in the form of problems and worries. Perhaps truly, they are the spice of life, in the absence of which life would become mundane and monotonous leaving us as an arrogant and rude person. I think, even if I was married to Carol, there would be no less problems coming than what it is presently are. See, when I am not having Carol in my life, I am sad thinking about her decision to marry me that whether she will agree or refuse. When she will marry me, I would still have to fight with my fear of losing her due to any disease. Perhaps she would have asked for divorce and would marry another man if I will prove to be a loser in life on which my condition would have been more miserable than today. Maybe she would slip on the floor and get her legs fractured and would become handicapped forever.

However I would have loved Carol with the same depth of emotions even if she would have become handicapped losing her legs forever. I would have accepted her with all her pain and shortcomings. But, I am sure that this is not the case with Carol. I can't anticipate what will happen, whether she will support me during the darkest phase of my life or just leave quietly.

And, for Carol, I am ready to tolerate everything and anything. But, if it would have been done by someone else, I would have accused him for his selfish behaviour. It was my love for Carol that I would appreciate her even in her meanest form.

Someday if I'll get bankrupt and become penniless, and I go to Carol with my proposal and she refuses me, even then I will not complain. I will not blame her rather I will consider this as a wise decision. Nobody wants her life partner to be a loser. There is nothing wrong. But, if someday I'll become a rich and successful man and Carol becomes penniless, in such a situation too I'll remain the same Cyrus for her, craving for her love.

After having a deep contemplation about Carol, I fell asleep. I had a dream in which I saw Carol. We both were staying in a house. I was in the washroom, the two sides of which were fully covered by a clean mirror. I was wearing a black trouser with a blue T-shirt. I opened the washroom's door and asked Carol for the towel to dry my wet face. She came and handed me the towel. She was looking gorgeous in a navy blue cotton jeans and dark brown sweatshirt (with something written on it which I don't remember). I also saw a small boy, barely of two years old. He was playing with the toys and Carol was accompanying him. I heard Carol saying to that child, "Dad is in the washroom, my child". Next I saw Carol's parents sitting on the sofa. Carol was telling them, "It's the right time to get Isaac admitted to the school". Her parents also consented. I was watching the most wonderful dream of my life till someone suddenly knocked door and ruined it. I opened the door. There were the two regular men standing with a bucket filled with water, a phenol bottle, a broom and a dustbin. My sadness knew no bounds. I couldn't complete my dream. I wanted to see the dream further.

The dream made me emotional. I think, dreams are the best videos we can see and experience too. Also, sometimes, when we get ourselves over involved into something, it might take the form of a dream. It was a very sad moment. They entered my room and started their work. There was a third man cleaning the corridor outside the rooms. The door was open and the facial wishes with the students were on the go. I received a call from home which continued till the departure of the two men.

I went to my friend's place on the third floor. He was my classmate at the Daniel Institute. His name was Cobham Alessi. He was from

Bergamo, a city of Lombardy region of Italy. He was by nature a reticent. I guess, he had a wish to become a great father and a serious man too. He treated me like a son. I sometimes called him 'dad' being frustrated by his behaviour. He only listened to me and talked very little. You can say that I was Katie to him in terms of talking. I always started the conversation and ended it. I even complained for his nature but he was incorrigible. He was reclusive and avoided to mingle into the society. I think, he must have set his boundary around him which was quite tightly knitted having only selected people in his list. But the list of persons listening to him and bearing his father-like nature patiently was huge and perhaps I had enlisted my name at top of that list.

Reaching the floor of Cobham's room, I knocked the door. I used to knock his door as a form of courtesy towards him. On the contrary, he used to bang mine. He opened the door's lock but did not open the door and quickly moved to his bed. This was his usual habit. I entered. As usual, the same kind of smell of deodorants, books and hair gels welcomed me.

"How are you?", I asked in my usual tone. This was the beginning of our every meeting which had to be started by me always.

"Fine", he answered in one of the laziest tones of the world. For a few minutes, there was a complete silence in the room. My father-like friend, as usual, was unwilling to start the conversation. But if he speaks, he'll be sad whole day for that mistake.

Still he was much better than Peter. He talked with me frequently but not always. He had the habit of listening and nodding head. He had inspired me a lot with his valuable suggestions regarding studies.

After spending some time with Cobham I headed back to my room. I had some work as homework to be done, given by the teachers. I hurried to my bathroom for bathing. I always ensured that the second door's lock was closed otherwise I would have become a topic of laughter for the Room No. 3 boy and his friends.

Once Room No. 3 boy's mother saw me in an embarrassing state while entering the bathroom. Fortunately enough I was wearing underwear; otherwise, I would have been felt humiliated in front of her. She smiled and then slipped into her room quickly. When I met her at the hostel mess I was unable to even have an eye contact with her.

As soon as I started bathing, the chilled water gave me pain with its each drop pouring down from the mug. I wanted to wrap it up quickly. Coming out of the bathroom, I wiped out the body and head to dry. Then I dressed up, applied cream on my face and put oil on the head. Then, I sat on the chair to study. Few seconds might have been passed when suddenly I started to feel acute headache. Within next few seconds, it increased. It was so painful and strong that for a few second, I became almost blind. I was unable to see anything. It felt as though I lost the control over my brain losing my power of thinking. I felt as if I lost my memory. I was not even able to recall my name. Everything around me looked strange. I couldn't even identify the door instead I could see only a brown coloured rectangular object in front of me but I couldn't recognise it. I was almost dying with pain. For 10–15 minute, I remained holding the same position sitting on the chair with my head held down by two hands crying in pain.

Then I looked at my bed. Getting up from the chair, I went to the bed laming on the floor. I eased myself on the bed. The headache was still there. I fell asleep after some time. When I woke up, I found myself in a new world welcoming me . . . . a world where there was no happiness, no appreciation, continuous jeering and the occurrence of all sorts of mental illness.

I got up with difficulty and sat on the bed leaning against its back part. Till then, my headache had gone away. It felt quite relieved as a burden was off my head. I had forgotten what had happened to me. I could only remember that my head was severely aching, as if it would explode. But later on I remembered some scenes.

Gradually, I started to identify the things around me. Though my recalling power was being revived slowly, only a little recalling power was left within me. The rest had already vanished. But, I was unaware of the most dangerous thing coming towards me. I kept sitting on my bed comfortably. I didn't even want to move or do anything. I had lost my interest and desire in almost everything, neither I wanted to spend time with Katie and Simon, nor I had the desire to play games on Katie's mobile, nor to read about David and Billy on the internet, who were my role models.

Let me tell you about them. David, a legendary student of Daniel Institute, was doing engineering from MIT which was my dream destination. Billy was a Harvard University graduate from where I dreamt to do MBA. I had not even seen Harvard University in my life and he was its graduate, so it was a big thing for me. Some of my friends had discussed in the class about few of their friends who got the opportunity to study at MIT and Harvard. Both of them were my dreamlands for higher education. Hence, I was naturally inclined towards MIT and Harvard with David and Billy being my role models. Moreover, some of my acquaintances appreciated the students selected in MIT and Harvard. There were some students senior to me with whom I was in good talking terms. They were selected in MIT. I didn't know anyone personally who was selected in Harvard. Though I wanted to be a MITian but more than that I wanted to experience how it felt to be like Billy. I admired him more than David.

I used to read about David and Billy on the internet. As the whole world searched and read about eminent personalities like Abraham Lincoln, Bill Gates, Steve Jobs and others, I was stuck to these two people. I used to search about them on Katie's mobile. Even though it appeared funny to her, she never showed any sign of it. I used to tell her – 'They are my role models and I dream to meet them someday in life. For me, they are the legend. They are bigger than any celebrity on earth for me.'

KATIE PROPOSES ME

I WAS NEITHER a good nor a true lover. In fact, I never tried to be a one.

Sometimes, you do not understand the importance of valuable things around you until you lose them; consequently, you do your own loss. You should be grateful that there is someone in your life who loves you. You should feel fortunate that you have somebody you can trust and will always support you. In your success, he is there to celebrate it with you multiplying your happiness. While you are sad, his mere presence can reduce your sadness. Their absence makes us realise their true importance in our life during the adverse situations or when you are left alone. When you decide to kill yourself, at that moment, he will come to you and try to comfort you in spite of your ignorance towards him. You may turn your eyes away from him and ask him to leave. In spite of the fact that you need some time alone to come back to normal state, he will try all his means to console you. You may even lose your temper on him but he will even kill his ego for you. You reject them thousands of times but still they pursue you to eat. But we don't get their real intention which is nothing more than our happiness. What will he get if you eat the food? Will he get a promotion in his job? Will he get gold or silver? Will he get any kind of benefit from this? Is he doing it for himself? No, it's just his love for you that is compelling him to chase you. They want you to prosper, become successful in life and be a bright positive person. They can't tolerate your downfall or you being deteriorated from your standards unlike other envious people who would rather enjoy seeing you degrading. But those who care for you seem to take your troubles at their heart.

You should take the depth of his love into consideration with the most politeness. You should never forget that there are some pitiful souls out there who do not have even a single person who cares for them. They just sit in their room keeping the lights off and suffocate themselves in their anxiety and depression. They don't care about time or people around them and get immersed into darkness where mostly they are alone. This depression eats them alive and causes physical frailty as well as mental recklessness in them. It affects their immunity system and let any disease attack them easily. Perhaps, they have already been affected by the disease of loneliness. They are already bearing the disease of loveless life. They never call anyone nor does anyone call them. If, rarely, any call comes in their way, they talk so less or sometimes so rudely to the person (on the other side of the phone) that he never thinks about calling again in the future. After finishing the call, they cry at their own mistake and curse themselves. The same behaviour they repeat with their guests. Hence, like phone calls, the entry of guests also is restricted in their life. More than half of their guests stop visiting them because they never care about attending any invitation neither they go to their place. They seclude themselves from the society ignoring almost every type of interactions. The little chance of communication with the society rests upon their opportunity with the people in office, school, college or business dealings, which also comes to be nullified soon when they stop involving even with them.

If he is a college student, then he will spend hours sitting beside the window leaning against the wall or lying on the bed as a paralysed patient. Sometimes, he will sit on the carpet of the floor with his back resting on a corner of his bed and rotating things whichever are nearer to him. He plays games non-stop on his laptop. He will keep searching something or the other on the internet which can divert and interest him. He will look for the news of any break-up happening between love birds to mitigate his pain and go through the moment of purgation which can relieve his ache for a few moments acknowledging the fact that the whole world is playing the same game of betrayal. He will turn down any offer to attend any party even with his parents. He will ignore his friends too by instructing his family members to lie about his presence at home if any of his friends asks for him. In case of further inquiry about his arrival by friends, he also instructs them to say, "I don't know. He had not told about the timing before leaving the house".

When he is assured of their departure, he will feel very relieved and will praise his loneliness and will spend time alone till he wants to. His approach towards the world becomes negative. He starts to despise any relation with human being who as per his observation is cruel, mean, money minded and deceitful. He begins to hold the notion that the world salutes the person who has a lot of wealth which can be fairly supported by the quotations like 'Victory has hundred fathers but defeat is an orphan'. Such quotations will give his pervert thoughts the acceleration required to run towards the wrong directions. During such moments, the sayings like 'Be kind', 'Be generous', 'Be merciful', 'Love all Hate none', 'Friendship is the golden chain', 'We are all brothers and sisters' do not carry logic anymore. Even if these positive thoughts pay visit to his mind, instead of paying heed to them, he will try to modify them like 'Be cruel', 'Never be generous', 'Be merciless', 'Hate all Love none', 'Friendship is the rusted chain', 'We are neither brothers nor sisters'. He will believe that we have been programmed to hurt others and 'we are the life-taking enemies of each other'. If the girlfriend of this guy shows her attitude of self-attention, then in terms of revenge she'll be taught a life-long lesson by him which can't be described in words. As a result, the poor girl will run after him and will try to please him; she will surrender herself to him and vow an undying loyalty to him, or in fact not dare to show her attitude to him. I disliked such attitude in people the most and hated it terribly. Neither the boy nor the girl should chase one another rather they should understand that the true bond actually lies in mutual understanding and forgiveness which certainly increases love for one another.

If the person is married, then he will behave differently. He will return home just to fight. Even if you lift him up on your shoulders, it can't calm him down, and his wife will be the first victim and will have to face the worst. He will find reasons to fight with her. If she needs rest after performing the daily household chores then it becomes easier for him to create violence. They start fighting over the preparation of food.

The husband is in search of the right time. He will wait for his wife to ask him for help in cooking. He is impatient due to which he is unable to wait. He is sitting on the sofa. The wife has no idea about the poisonous arrow about to be triggered towards her. She comes near the sofa tying her hair and almost orders, "I'm very tired today. Please make the whole food. I can't even stand properly. Go fast and make the food. I'm very hungry". Ah! What a fuel has been added to the already lit fire. Today the husband is not in the same good mood of which she is unaware. She doesn't know what he will do. He was already unwilling to eat, forget about cooking for both himself and his wife. Then, a cold war begins between them. Money takes the centre position in this fight. The divided budget of money is declared. 'You should be satisfied with what you have' becomes the slogan of this fight. For initial few days, the self-respect takes the front seat. Both of them burn themselves in the fire of hatred mixed with resentment. Later on, the dispute is settled down due to the initiative taken by one of them to mend the relation. In case both are super egoistic, then the news of splitting up soon spreads everywhere resulting into their divorce.

You don't damage your self-esteem by asking for apology to somebody who deserves your apology. In fact, the person becomes superior, in dignity. But I think it is rational when both the parties are guilty to their mistakes.

Forgiving others is one of the greatest virtues of a human character. If you are not strong enough to forgive the small mistakes of others, how can you expect others to forgive your big mistakes!

If the wife is a bit extravagant, then the husband scolds, "You are wasting the money to maintain your luxurious life. Do you know how the money is earned? No, but you know how to waste it like water!". On the contrary, if the husband's greatest happiness lies in the fulfilment of the desires of his wife, he says, "Lead a luxurious life. Just think if I don't earn it for you, then for whom I earn! The money is for you only, my dear!".

Perhaps loneliness affects our speech to the extent that we start to neglect the emotions of others and speak harshly which breaks their heart.

Unlike these people, I ensured that no one should get hurt by my decision of living a reclusive life. I am not in favour of treating others badly or insulting them due to my sadness.

I had called Katie while sitting on the bed. She arrived within five minutes. She was just a call away from me whenever I needed her.

As she entered, I couldn't see into her eyes as I was shameful for my deeds. In spite of that, she was ready to help me without any qualms and with the same love and devotion.

Inside of me, I was struggling and cursing myself. It was painful. As I looked at Katie, tears rolled down my cheeks. It was certainly unbearable for her to watch me in such state. She quickly came towards me and sat beside me. She wanted to envelop me into her arms like a mother does to her child. But, keeping my warnings in mind, she restrained herself. Tears were unstoppable and were wetting my costly sweatshirt completely. She was continuously asking about my reason to cry but I had no answer. I was just crying continuously.

She let me cry for a few minute and did not ask anything. In the meantime, she broke her silence and asked me to stop crying. She said that she was not able to bear my pain. She didn't want me to feel annoyed so she didn't interrupt and waited for my tears to stop.

It took too long for me to control my tears as they were the indication of the intensity of my pain inside.

I could never imagine that I could be so mean towards somebody who cares for me so much.

After some time, I got the hold on myself and stopped crying. I was contemplating on the purpose of my life. Katie waited patiently for me to utter few words at least.

"See, your big eyelashes are so wet now", she said wiping my tears with her new handkerchief because fingers would not be comfortable to clean. She went ahead, "Now tell me, why were you crying? I had not expected this from you, Cyrus". I was silent and rested myself on the back part of the bed. Then I kept my chin on my knees and started looking in forward direction. She then said, "Cyril, I can't bear you being sad. But, today I saw you weeping bitterly as a child. Your tears wetted your shirt. Not even the bullet can hurt me so hard than what your tears did, Cyrus. When your eyes were crying, my heart was aching and crying too, and that too much more than your eyes, Cyril. These tears should not come out again".

I realised that it was not right to be in that state. I calmed myself somehow and again leaned against the bed. Katie smiled. She knew that I didn't want any kind of physical contact until and unless we were married. I too smiled back at her.

For the first time, I saw Katie showing me a motherly love. This was a different kind of love a love between a young boy and a girl much older and mature to him.

Katie said, "Cyril, I don't care what you think, but it would be a pleasure to have you in my arms. Your body appears very soft to me. Though you are wafer thin, still your body will surely be very tender and smooth to touch. I had a little experience in the auditorium but you were afraid then. Without fear, it's going to be an adventure and an experience of heart's content. I wish if you were my husband, I would have got the chance to explore you more". She further added, "If only you permit me to cuddle you . . . . I ". I smiled at that.

She said, "Oh! Sorry, Cyrus. I forgot to ask you about your problem. I'm very sorry. So what happened to you?".

I replied, "As I sat down to study, I was attacked with a severe headache. It was deadly. In fact, it was a fatal experience for me". Then I told her the whole story. She got anxious but still maintained her composure quite well because she knew that I was afraid of hypersensitive people. She looked grave while listening to me.

"So, you are unable to visualise the things? You can't recall anything and can't recognise things even if it is kept in front of you". Katie repeated trying to confirm what was actually panicking me.

"No, slightly different from this! I'm giving you an example. Like, if you ask me to check whether the tap in the washroom is closed or not, I'll not be able to judge whether it is opened or closed. I'll keep standing there looking at it but won't be able to figure out what to do. If you ask me to give you some amount of money, I'll not be able to find out whether the coin I am giving you is of 1$ or 5$. At the same time, I am also disorientated about the things taking place around me.

Sadness could be seen on her face listening to my story. But no doubt, somewhere in her heart, the desire to marry me was whirling. In spite of being sad after listening to me, she did not forget to use her mind for convincing me to marry her. She said, "Now it seems like your dream of qualifying the MIT entrance will be very difficult to be fulfilled".

I became perturbed. She then said, "Don't worry, Cyril. I'm there to help you. I will fight against all your problems. I'm always there to support you. I'll help you in each and every way possible. I'll definitely help you in cracking the MIT entrance exams, and if you'll work hard along with me, one day you'll be there studying in order to achieve your dreams. I think I have got this most important responsibility to guide you. I feel very fortunate. But there is one problem; I can't touch you. If we want our communication to be good and bond strong, there should not be any wall between us. It is not only your dream but my mission too. Now I have involved myself in your dream so it's mine. There are certain problems which can't be explained or solved from distance. Cyril, I think you have understood what I mean to say and I hope you will take the right decision. Cyril, some problems have physical therapy as its remedy. Like a hug with your wife can heal many wounds and cure all sorts of ailments . . . . Perhaps you can see a wife . . . . in . . . . me. Then . . . . our communication will be much better and open. In fact, our relation will be propelled to the next level and will also boost your efforts. I'm not forcing you but you can take it as a piece of advice from a friend. I'll co-operate with you in every situation. I will shower all my love upon you if you choose me as your life partner . . . . Talking with you about love is of no use . . . . okay, forget that, forget it. I . . . . I mean to say that your dream of studying in MIT will become easier to achieve. I know to marry at this age and in this situation is difficult for you. It is going to be a tough decision for you. But trust me, Cyril, I'll never disappoint you. I know your age is not right to have a family but I'm there for support. I'll always be by your side no matter what happens. We'll both work hard to provide our child a bright future. I'll take the whole responsibility of our child. Cyril, we'll lead a very happy life. Imagine Cyril, you, me and our child living happily in our house. We'll eat, sleep and work together. Unlike today, no tension will harass our minds. Happiness will be showered upon us from raindrops". She almost hypnotised me giving me the glimpse of my future and asked me to imagine myself, her and our child living happily in a house. I rather imagined Carol in place of her. It's true that I started loving Katie but my love for Carol had not lessened down even a bit. No matter whoever comes to visit my life, they all were just guests, but when Carol used to meet me, I only craved for her and thought only about her. After a while, I replied, "Okay. I'm ready for it for the sake of my career and especially for MIT. But I'm only twelve now. However, the scientific research shows that getting married at such an early age is detrimental for the health of boys. I'm afraid if any serious disease occurs". Katie had read my face while I was thinking about the answer. She understood that I'd definitely agree to her.

Katie was shocked to know my age. In utter surprise, she said, "You're just twelve years old! So young! You know, I'm eighteen. We have six years of age difference. Cyril, you look like a ten-year-old boy. I thought it's just the matter of facial structure. But now, I'm really surprised to hear the truth. Cyril, you are very young. You'll have a tough time". She smiled at this and continued further, "But don't you worry, I'll manage it. You need not fear. I also don't expect you to be like a twenty-one-year-old man. I just want to bridge any gap setting us apart and will cross all the hurdles kept between you and me. I know, you are not that strong and mature but at least I'll get to kiss you". She gave a naughty smile but returned to her normal self quickly so that I do not consider her smile as a symbol of deceit and cunningness. 'Deceiving' in the sense that she was just looking forward to fulfil her desires, whereas she had told me that she wanted to do it for my good. 'Deceiving' here does not imply her selfish or deceptive nature. She was, undoubtedly, the best person I had ever met in my life. Not even Simon, my very first and the only true friend, could match her loyalty and devotion towards a relation. Before meeting her, I could only imagine a person like her to be in my life, somebody even better than Simon. Now I had got one in reality. My consideration, that Katie is better than Simon, itself proved her sheer dedication for me.

I said, "So, I'm ready for it. When are we going to marry?". Katie felt elated at this. It was unbelievable for her. Although the whole agreement of marriage was done quite a while before I said, 'I'm ready', my consent to this proposal just served as a final touch to everything. Unable to bear the happiness, tears rolled down her cheeks which was apparently the very symbol of her affection to me. But she succeeded in restoring her normal composure within few second. She moved a little backward, away from me and in a delicate voice, "Thank you, Cyril. I'll always be grateful to you. From now onwards till the marriage, I'll control my feelings of lust for you. I'll just suppress it into me only". I tried to tease her a little, saying, "You're looking very changed. How did such a sudden change come to you? What's the matter? I can't understand. What has happened to you?". She replied confidently, "If I'll not come close to you, will not talk to you about love, not touch or try to kiss you, then I'll feel a sort of emptiness in my soul; similar to a situation in which a box full of chocolates is kept in front of a child but he has been strictly instructed not to touch it till the completion of his school work. But it's okay! I'll develop a feeling of detachment. Then I'll crave for your love . . . . will long for you. I'll be eagerly waiting to have my mouth all over your lips. Our separation will make our love deeper for each other. And, that love will be pure, true and everlasting, the love, achieved after burning two souls together in the same fire of control over lust.

She then went forward to fix the date of marriage. Surprisingly, the date was the next day. She even took the responsibility of deciding the place of our marriage. She advised that the wedding will be in the presence of her family.

I think her marriage had nothing to do with my headache. Even if I was not suffering with my headache, even then she would have proposed me in some or the other way at any time. I felt as if my headache gave her the golden opportunity to accomplish her own desire.

At the same time, even I was glad to move forward on the path leading me to my dreams. Katie ordered in a humble way, "But first, we'll go to doctor for your check-up. After returning, we'll get married in the presence of parents and William. I spoke to them about it. They got excited and were very happy knowing that finally I found my life partner but they were astonished with your age. Still I think they will not have any problem with our marriage. It's just your decision for which we are waiting".

I expressed my concern for her, "Will the people not object to this wedding? You can be in trouble then". She firmly replied, "Leave the people. Don't worry about that. What's wrong if you're getting married? When our parents are not having any problem with this wedding, so why would anyone else have? If you're ready then there's no problem. It's you who'll decide. If you want to marry, nobody can stop you. We'll do it very secretly. We'll not let any government official know about it. And, if still they come to know, my parents will handle them. When you're ready, then maybe the officials won't have any objections . . . . You . . . . You just get prepared for the wedding". I did not like what she said but preferred to remain silent. The day was very lucky for me because we were having our vacation started from the very next day. When she asked me about my classes, I revealed to her about the holidays which were scheduled for 12 days. It was quite lengthy in order to give us time to refresh ourselves before beginning of another hectic work. Katie then took me to her house and introduced me to her parents.

Her parents were looking very happy. But they also looked surprised at their daughter's choice.

MASTER CYRUS AND MRS. KATIE

THAT EVENING, KATIE came to pay visit in my room. We both were heading towards New York for our wedding. I couldn't understand why she was so desperate and couldn't wait for a few days. I mean, the next day was too early in my opinion. The excitement might even have made her sleepless all the night. But perhaps the fear of spoiling the wedding day would have made her sleep; after all, it's the biggest day for her.

The next morning, Katie woke up early and came to my room. Here, the term 'my room' doesn't imply that I owned it. Actually it was one of the rooms I was staying in Katie's house. Katie had brought me to her home.

Like every time in the hostel, Katie knocked the door in the same familiar and humble manner. When you are full of humble thoughts, it is expressed in your every move and activity. Her humbleness used to please me as well as mesmerise me to a great extent because she used to behave with me normally despite of having a rich lineage. Though she was habitual to live amidst all sorts of luxury in a large bungalow, she never pointed out any defect or expressed her uneasiness or made faces while being with me in my room which was much inferior to that of her. She never refused to eat the foods which were not even of her level. I belonged to rich class family but it was nothing in front of her wealth.

Moreover, I never felt inferior to her because she never let me feel so. The most special thing I loved about her was that she inspired me to live my life again with great enthusiasm.

In the absence of a stoic meaning of your life, you find yourself on the verge of ending it. Falling in love is easier than loving someone. I had fallen in love with Carol but was trying to love Katie. Both the scenarios are quite different from each other. Falling in love attaches us to the person at the soul level, whereas trying to love a person who has fallen for us indicates the fact that we are neither attached to him nor love him. In spite of our numerous trials, we fail to love them the way they deserve. I had fallen for someone who had never reciprocated the same love to me that I gave her.

My affection for Carol had increased to a level where I lost my interest in everything, including life itself. I always felt lethargic. My laziness was due to the fact that I was not mentally fit. It did not even allow me to climb up the stairs. I was unable to ride my bicycle. I lost all my friends though they were not loyal and true but their company used to provide me much comfort than Carol's who was indifferent to all my sufferings.

My love for Carol was acting more like a venomous attack on my life. It became toxic for me. What was the use of running after a girl who can't make me happy? What was the use of craving for the girl who always ignores me, avoids me and never speaks to me? On the other hand, Katie proved her never-ending love for me. It is better to be with a girl who loves you, who will always stand by you during your difficulties and will never leave you alone if you fail. So, it was better to be with Katie. It doesn't matter much whether I would be able to love Katie or not but at least I would have a wife who'll love me. In addition, my company will make her happy too. My life taught me a lesson that we should spend our lives with the person who loves us as he is like a gift for us. He'll support us and will never harm us.

It's important to ensure at the very beginning that the girl whom you love also loves you back; otherwise, the result always turns out to be a painful misery. Even if she accepts your proposal, she'll make you run after her throughout your life. It will become more of a chasing game rather than a happy married life. She'll never entertain good feelings for you in her heart. She'll always want to remove her hurdle, which is you, from her way. In extreme cases, the consequences can be fearful. In spite of being your wife, she will always crave for her real love. She'll hardly look happy in your company. No matter how sweetly she smiles at you, the real story will remain hidden from you. You can never understand her or read her mind. Your marriage will symbolise a wooden stick continuously eaten by termites. Whatsoever you do to please her, you can never win her love for yourself. Most of the time, you'll be tricked by her false pretence which will slowly make you feel lifeless and dead inside. Your life will become a burden for you. You'll start sharing your problems with your close friends, relatives or office colleagues in a very negative way. You'll say – 'Life is a curse. The dead ones are luckier than us because they're free from the worldly problems. I want my children to get a job and get married too. After that I won't have any reason left with me to live'. These men are also committing suicide which is a bit different of kind. They are not committing suicide in reality but surely they are having a burning desire to finish themselves. Social reputation has no role to play here as a catalyst but the reason behind this is their deep rooted fear of life.

Many young married men say that their relationship with their wives is not cordial. All of them feel their wives to be a big problem, though publicly they say that they love their families and their wives very much. They are wrong. How can these two things occur at the same time? How can you love and hate the same person at the same time? They just speak like this for the sake of their dignity in the society. They don't really love their wives. Their wives too might not be loving them which is not a big deal for them since every human being is of different nature that might not match with every human you meet in your life. Many a times, we see that couples are not compatible and both are opposite in nature which adds fuel to the fire and makes their small trouble bigger causing stress in relation.

People who grumble about their married life that they are frustrated with their wives but still love them are actually lying because the true love always increases and never fades away. Your each day becomes a blessing for you. You feel the pleasure of your relationship every day. While being in the office, you will constantly think about your home and will eagerly wait for the office hours to get over so that you can go back to your home as soon as possible. No matter how hard the situation becomes, you will still feel each day of your marriage as the first day. On the other hand, what we witness around us is people distributing sweets among the friends, relatives and colleagues on some day only to spend the rest of their lives slogging and shedding tears. It really saddens me.

Your promotion at the workplace or a lot of money are not the only reason to make your life happier. Because it might happen that some of your colleagues do not get promotion for years, but does that mean the non-promoted ones are not living a happy life? Or happiness has gone away from their lives forever? It's not like that. We should not become the nagging person who complains about everything of his life, especially family members or wife. If you had to complain only, about your wife, you should not have married her.

In my opinion, my would-be-wife, Katie, was different from everyone. We could think about our married life to be successful; in fact, we were confident and determined to lead a happy life forever. We had a high compatibility. We hardly fought with each other. When both husband and wife love each other truly and madly, they'll ignore each other's mistake and rather look for solutions and co-operate with each other. Fights take place in the relations which are built on weak foundations. But, I think, I was very lucky to get a wife like Katie who understood me as well as respected my feelings more than anyone had.

"Cyril, I have taken appointment from Claudia Lois's clinic. She's a neurologist. I have decided to consult with her about your health. You'll be alright in a few days", Katie said. Our marriage was scheduled to be solemnised at night. This awkward request was made by me as I didn't want to marry during the daytime. It's not the matter of auspicious timing. It's just that during the day, lights and colourfulness can't be enjoyed, whereas night would be perfect for such celebrations. Katie's family agreed to my idea because she convinced them. Perhaps, Katie was not much concerned about the timing of the marriage. For her, I was of more importance. I, marrying her, was enough for her. Moreover, I guess, night would be more exciting for her as she wouldn't have to wait after marriage to jump and get flattened on me on the bed.

When the preparation was on progress, Katie's parents always put all the burden of responsibilities on Katie previously being given to me by Katie's brother. They always said, "Cyrus is very small. He can't handle this job. Katie, you do this work. How will he do it?". Katie did all the jobs on behalf of me, no matter how small the they were. But the major work was being performed by the workers. We were doing just a little bit and that too the planning ones. Katie's parents had arranged the whole programme in a very private manner. I wondered if everything has to be done privately, then what is the use of decorating the house? Katie told me that only interior of the house will be decorated, among which her bedroom is going to be the best. Moreover, none would be able to anticipate seeing the decoration whether the celebration is of marriage or of someone's birthday.

She had asked her parents to let both of us take some time out for ourselves. So we both sat together on the two separate single-seated sofas. She sat on the other sofa covering almost the whole of it. She was not an obese. She was physically fit. The fact is that even her normal physique was much bigger than any normal person. Now, she maintained a considerable distance from me. She knew that it was not going to last long, so she made her mind to align herself with my chastity.

"Cyril, how are you feeling?", she enquired.

"Good", I replied with a smile.

She went ahead, "I'm very happy. I don't have words to express my happiness. From tomorrow you'll be mine". She continued further, "At 10:30 am, we'll go to the doctor. Your appointment is at 11:00 am. It's a . . . . it's a less than fifteen-minute run from here. I hope, your problem is not so serious but still we have to consult".

I was pondering over something and was looking here and there. Whenever my eyes met with Katie's, we both smiled at each other. Katie seemed to be of an easy and placid disposition because she did not want to disturb me. She was staring at me. Though not uttering any word, the happiness was clearly visible over her face. At the same time, she was calm too.

We should feel the happiness inside of us and never express it in an exciting manner. Your happiness or sadness will be flashed over your face. Your sadness can't remain hidden for long; in spite of your numerous trials of wearing a fake smile on your face, it will be revealed. Perhaps, there are some people trained in the field of hiding emotions well behind their smile. But, I think, even a proficient person can't hold it for long enough to misguide others. There is always a fear of degradation from inside. In doing so, they'll become hollow from inside, and their suppression can cause them to break down at any time, sometimes at the cost of their life due to heart failure.

In my opinion, an unreasonable smile can't allow happiness. On the contrary, it's the happiness that brings the smile on our face. The acts of laughing with no reason leads your heart to become unemotional. Perhaps, smiling is the better option than laughing. Fake smiles can definitely misguide people but you can't hide the truth from yourself.

When you are happy and content, the sense of forgiveness comes naturally to you, and you take initiative in the humanitarian grounds with a motto of uplifting the inferiors and helping the needy. But the sadness in you will attract negative and morally pervert thoughts to you.

Katie was happy within her heart. She was experiencing the true pleasures of her life.

Katie interrupted my thoughts. She asked me to come to her room which was on the first floor. She wanted to have a talk with me with no one around us. I was fatigued because I had not had enough sleep last night. I was climbing up the stairs feeling very lazily and sluggish, sticking to the railing and sometimes clinging to it. William was observing me from a distance. He came to my assistance and detached me from the railing whenever I attached myself to it. My repeating act irked him to the extent that he picked me up in his arms and took me to Katie's room. Throwing me gently on the bed, he went away. Perhaps, he did this because he didn't want Katie's schedule to get spoiled. He might have already known that I didn't want Katie to get physical with me.

"Go to sleep, Cyril. You're looking very tired", Katie advised. I smiled at her and said, "I'll just rest. I'll not sleep". She smiled and nodded at my childish silliness as she knew that I would sleep. It was my habit to say 'I would rest and not sleep' but eventually I used to sleep struggling with myself not to do so.

I covered my whole body with blanket including the back of my head leaving only my face visible outside with a little part of the head uncovered. My hairs were unevenly scattered on my forehead. "Looking like a doll. So cute!", Katie said as she blushed. Holding herself back, she continued, "Now go to sleep. I'm going from here or else I'll commit a mistake again. I'm unable to control the urge. I have to go from here. Enjoy the sweet sleep, my little child". She gave a motherly affectionate smile and left.

Since Katie had brought me to her home without an early intimation, I had not brought my other set of clothes from my room. She did not give the least attention to it, she had her complete focus on me.

After some time I woke up and took bath. Katie gave me some new pairs. I did not want her to search for my clothes in my room, so I agreed to join her in her hasty journey without any question.

After dressing up, I applied oil on my head. But still, instead of getting freshened, I was feeling sleepy. The long conversation with Katie had created the whole mess. When you have not slept properly last night and you're trying to compensate that in the morning after having a bath, it's not going to make you feel rejuvenated and would rather be a painful one. You'll feel attacked by all the weaknesses of the world in your tiny little body. And, if you'll repeat it on a daily basis, you'll become vulnerable to any sort of illness. Hence, I decided not to repeat it again.

Soon I fell asleep. It was a very sweet sleep . . . . a sleep without any tension or fear . . . a sleep which has only sweet dreams . . . a sleep that can freshen you up and reduce the mental troubles capable to push you to the edge of committing suicide. All the characteristics of that sleep were very beneficial to my physical as well as mental health.

The word 'suicide' had got deeply engraved into my psyche. The first solution that ever came to my mind for my troubles in extreme sadness was that I should kill myself. I think, the reason behind such solution was my immature brain that couldn't find any other effective solution except that. I think, my cowardice always dominated my courageous feelings or maybe I was a timid who always chose to cover his face and avoided to look into troubles, instead of facing it bravely.

A person taking recourse of committing suicide to put an end to his pain has already experienced an extreme of emotions. It's very hard to describe the intensity of his pain. Being emotionally drained, the feelings of delight and demise seemed to have no difference. During such state, even the arrival of any celebrity at his home wouldn't surprise him. He will exhibit no interest even at the dinner invitation at place of any celebrity. But not only that, even the sight of a person lying dead in a pool of blood can't stir him emotionally. All such emotionally distant behaviour in him is actually due to the fact that his dark emotions have created a void within him which has made him completely lost in his own worries not bothering about others and at the same time affecting his heart. This is perhaps because he thinks that his own life is filled with sorrow so why should he take interest in others. Such people remain indifferent to the materialistic possession of life and do not pay heed to even the showering of gold and silver. His sole aim of life revolves around only one thought i.e. how to commit suicide. His urge of reaching his aim is so high that through which he can startle even a successful person. In fact, sometimes, the ambition of that successful person can't match the strong drive of the person who is about to commit suicide. He has got a different type of energy and power in him . . . . a power which can overshadow almost anyone and overcome his hurdles. This power reaches to its peak just before he is about to end his life. But sadly enough, when he ends his life, it disappears along with him and the world remains unaware of it. He becomes one of the most unlucky people of the world 'unlucky' in the sense that he got everything but could not find the purpose of his life and couldn't enjoy what he has been endowed with. He could not use his power in the most healthy way. In fact, he could not identify that power which had developed in him since the time he decided to commit suicide till he was about to commit it. On the contrary, the successful person can rationalise the power generated in him even at the most negative moment of his life; whatsoever or how powerful it may be, It may be lesser than the power of the person who has suicidal tendency. Still he recognises it at the very moment and put it to use in a healthy manner. The power described here is not at all hypothetical. It is due to the intensity of sadness which instils within them such an enormous power. We should always remember that none else but we are responsible for our sadness and troubles; if anybody else is responsible for it then he is liable to be punished. Life allows us to commit mistakes which most of us do surely in life, but with this a responsibility too is given to us that is to learn from our own mistakes and turn it into our step towards success, our weapon to fight with the adversities of life. I think, it is very rare to perceive it in someone; only strong personalities are able to use their sadness as a ladder to reach the success. In sadness, you will perform your work with concentration which does not imply that happiness reduces your concentration. Concentration is a kind of virtue which will be under your control if only you know the way of channelizing your own sadness towards a positive direction. But if you are a type of person who keeps whining about your sadness to others and attracting people to you for sympathy for the whole day, then it shows that you are not prudent to use your sadness for your own benefit. It will automatically generate a feeling of sadness afterwards. The person who endures his sadness and pain quietly and keeps patience even in the most difficult situation is the one capable of making use of his own sadness. If you are sad, it becomes challenging for almost anyone to make you happy. At most, you will give a fake smile and that smile will hurt you in return. The same condition applies to the person who is about to commit suicide. Your any tickling or attack on him will be fruitless. His sadness will overcome the effect of your attack. Tickling can make a person laugh who is already happy and leads a normal life. But a sad person is much like a vessel filled with the liquid of sadness which can't be shaken to yield a desired effect.

"Cyril, come. It's the time to go", William said waking me up from my sound sleep. I was feeling so sleepy that I could hardly hear his voice. He did it very carefully. He first gently embedded his finger into my feet then shook it. I got to know about it when he told me after I woke up. Due to his gentleness, I did not feel the pain of sudden break of sleep. I think the effect on the feet had slowly migrated into the brain. Since I was feeling tired, I slept again. He again tried to wake me up but I got stuck to the bed. I wrapped my whole body with the blanket leaving the face as I always preferred not covering it. But he was determined to break my sleep and even tried to get the blanket off me. Sadly his all attempts went in vain. At last, he picked me up along with the blanket and took me over his shoulder.

"Okay, I'm getting up", I said loudly. He left me. I took my standing position. I uncovered myself and kept the blanket on the bed.

"Go to washroom and wash your face. I'm bringing the clothes", he said and headed outside. Seeing him leaving, I again jumped on the bed. But I was unaware of the other side of William's nature; he suddenly turned around, moved to the bed, pulled my legs and picked me up. He then took me to the washroom and forcibly got my face washed. He took out a new soft towel from the wardrobe and wiped my face. It was not easy for him to take out that towel because on the other hand he was managing to have a tight hold on me as I was struggling to get out of his arms. He then asked Katie on call to bring my clothes. Till then, he was carrying me in his arms.

When he wiped my face after the wash, I was looking very charming. "What a beautiful face!", he said, as he tried to control himself. He tried to take his fixed eyes away and looked at other directions but again his eyes were travelling back towards me. At last, he couldn't subdue his urge and his patience gave up. He lifted me up near his lips and kissed me on my cheek. I could feel the moisture of his kiss on my cheek which was a sign of his uncontrolled impulsive nature. It also showed the purity of his love towards me. At last, we both smiled at each other. I was quite comfortable in his arms so I closed my eyes and stuck to him. If any person would have seen us, he would have said that a father is lovingly carrying his child in his arms. He truly looked like a father to me. The eight-year difference between us could easily be noticed in our maturity level and our physique.

I don't know what had attracted Katie towards me which made her fall in love with me (either as a mother or as a girlfriend). Her love resembled much with motherly affection than like girly attraction. She was always very lenient with me. When she looked at me, it looked as though I'm her child. She never behaved badly nor fought with me. She always agreed on everything with me and never refused.

Katie was a like a mother who loves her child so much that she even hesitates to scold him fearing that he might fall into depression. She fears that her son might start abhorring her company. She always found an alternate solution to improve her kids. She would make her son understand anything with love and not by force.

There are some mothers who love their kids a lot but can thrash them black and blue when they are angry on them. They are definitely very different from Katie. They can't even tolerate a little sadness on their children's face, forget about the tears. This type of mothers are sensitive for their children. However, what I think is that when the child is on the track of being spoiled, a light beating can serve the purpose for sure.

Katie had always been very compassionate towards me and couldn't bear even a bit of sadness.

Katie came to my room with the clothes. She was shocked to see me in William's arms. "For a moment, I felt like you are his son", Katie said in an emotional tone. She continued, "If I would have been your mother, I would have been the luckiest person on earth".

I said, "Then you would not have got me as your husband. She smiled and said, "Oh! Then I wish that our son should be as cute as you or even more than you!".

William smiled at her thought. He said to Katie, "Cyrus was not getting up. He was jumping back again and again to bed after I woke him up. I had to forcibly get him off the bed and fresh him up".

"William, he's still a child and the one who needs enough sleep", Katie teased me. William nodded while smiling. "Today is his appointment with the doctor. I can't delay that. That's why I had to do all this. Honestly, it made me very uncomfortable. I was forced to do so. Cyrus will not understand this", William showed his concern for me.

"Enjoying in the arms", Katie joked, as William pulled my cheek. I was bashful. In fact, I always felt like that whenever I see two adults talking with each other in my presence. "Okay, I'm going. I have to see the other preparations of marriage too", William said and then putting me down on sofa, he went off. After him seeing going, I comfortably rested myself on it.

Katie said, "Now change your clothes. We'll leave by 10:30 am".

I replied, "I'm going to dressing room. I'll change there". Katie knew that I had some different plans in my head already running. She knew I would lay down on the floor covered with a cushion and will fall asleep. Then, I would remain there for a long time. She knew that I would take her leniency as an advantage.

"No, you change your clothes here, in front of me", she ordered in a firm voice.

I replied, "I won't. I feel shy taking off my clothes in front of anyone. I will go to the dressing room only". She said, "I know, it's beyond your moral ethics. I knew it, Cyril. I'm not watching you. I'll close my eyes. I'll not see you changing your clothes See, I've closed my eyes. Now, you can change".

I said, "I don't have trust on anyone. You are closing your eyes now but you can open them when I'll take off all my clothes or maybe you'll see the whole scene with slightly opened eyes. I don't have trust on you too. My friend had fooled me like this once when he had invited me to his birthday party". Now, Katie seemed to be irritated. She said, "You are wearing your vest and underwear. Why are you so shy? What will happen even if I see you like that? Not even a girl can compete you in the matter of coyness. Even the girls are not that much You simply don't understand anything.

Sometimes, you behave in such a stupid manner that I feel like thrashing you. When I'm telling you that I'll not open the eyes, I mean it . . . . Now, did you get me or should I make you understand in another language?". Katie had almost shouted on me and then ordered me to sit on the sofa.

This time she disappointed me. I did not reply anything and began to move towards almirah slowly. I started to unpack the new sweatshirt.

I began to develop a kind of fear in me. Such behaviour used to frighten me. I didn't expect such a response from Katie. I do understand that every human being is not devoid of follies in their nature and so was I but I paid for that in the form of distress and pain which persisted in my life for a long time. Katie wanted me to follow her instructions. Katie's behaviour hurt me, though I understood that she was not unreasonable with her demands. It was her love that was compelling her do the things she didn't want to. But, heart does not understand the intention of the other person. It just breaks. It just becomes sad and starts crying over the split milk. What the heart feels is manifested on the face itself. The pain in your heart snatches away the glow from the face and leaves it being morose. It can't be easily identifiable but can be explored by only who loves you. He can read your face. He can judge your fake smile. Katie was the most capable person who could have judged me. She too understood that by forcing her own will upon me, she had done wrong. She was feeling guilty. "Sorry, Cyrus. I spoke more than it required . . . . l I don't want you to dislike me", she confessed. She went to the dressing room, opened its door and silently indicated me to come over. I went inside but did not lie down. My sleep had gone away. I changed my clothes and came out. Katie was standing at the window pane looking outside. It was a large window pane. She was looking extremely sad. She was lost in some thoughts. The glow of her face had faded away. She had only scolded me but if anyone would have looked at her face, he would have said that Katie might have committed any serious crime.

I became sympathetic for her. I realised that I should not have been so rigid.

When somebody shows his love, he can't be taken for granted and can't be used to serve your own selfish motives. You should be considerate to his small mistakes without being angry; if it keeps happening, it may decrease his love for you like termites eating the wood. Small fights in love is tolerable and usually does not affect the relationship. You may have heard some couples saying that they fight with each other daily but then also they have immense love for each other. These fights are not small. These are the frightening ones. There are some husbands and wives who end up reconciling after such fights. They are in opinion of a thinking that love can overcome any shortcoming in their relation. But I am not a follower of such type of beliefs. What type of a love is this? If you both love each other then why do you fight? Loving and fighting taking place in a relationship., If It is so then it's strange. Is their love not strong enough to prevent them from fighting? If they would have loved each other so much, they would not have even showed anger in their eyes for each other. If you are fighting with your wife regularly, your love life is being affected somehow. It is weakening your trust and love for each other because fighting is an unhealthy issue which can bring you unpredictable consequences. It can also separate you from your better half and cause split between friends or the husband wife duo or relatives. The habit of wanting over-attention from our loved ones can take that person permanently away from us because he may get tedious of running behind us. I personally don't like this habit. But if they are important enough to your life, we should fight against all odds no matter how harsh it could be—parents, teachers or any good person are the ones who should be given such a selfless treatment. They deserve it. If there is a non deserving case, then we must avoid such selflessness, otherwise it can give us a life-long pain and distress.

I felt sad to see Katie standing quietly near the window pane. She looked like a poor man who has lost his only gold coin kept safely for quite a long time. She looked as if she had lost everything she had. She loved me the most and she herself became the reason of my annoyance; this thought exacerbated her problem even more. So it was surely a moment of mourning for her. She felt being left alone in cold.

I could feel her sadness standing away from her which helped me understand about my own feelings for her though I repeatedly rejected it. It gave an insight that loving someone doesn't depend on us, instead we fall in love unknowingly. Similarly I had fallen in love with Carol without realising that fact, and now It's Katie who really made me understand it.

I went near Katie. Seeing me advancing towards her, she turned her head and looked at me but she couldn't gather courage to look at me again. I stood by her side waiting for her to start conversation because I was feeling guilty for my rudeness. But how could she start it! She was already feeling guilty to even look into my eyes. Finally, I mustered up my courage and said, "I'm sorry . . . . I should not have stuck to my opinion . . . . I have hurt you. Katie, I'm very sorry for this. I know you get hurt but you will never say it . . . . neither you will complain. You always want me to be happy . . . . you are a nice person . . . . I . . . . I like you." Katie was blaming herself for the whole incident I think, she was unaware of my mistake. This is what you do if you love someone truly. You ignore his all mistakes and take the blame on yourself for any misunderstanding happening between you and him. That's why my words had surprised her to the core. She turned and looked at me. Her eyes were full of tears which must be the tears of happiness. But I didn't know whether the happiness emerged from the fact that I had forgiven her or I had accepted my mistake. Whatever be the reason, I was content to see her happy at last.

She had her eyes full of tears which were about to roll down the moment she would close them. The same thing happened. The moment she closed her eyes for a fraction of a second, tears made their paths on her cheeks. Then it was unstoppable. We all know that heart pumps the blood but this time it was pumping tears. She wanted to hug me tight but she curbed her desire. So, I gave her a pillow as my substitute. She smiled at my childish act and embraced the pillow assuming that it was me. The embracement accelerated the rate of rolling down of her tears. She held it as tight as she could. It acted like a pain reliever.

I wiped her tears with the clothes that I took off few minutes ago. For the first time, in my life, I wiped anyone's tears. She smiled and wiped off the rest by herself. She knew that I was uncomfortable doing it. After all, we had made a promise to ourselves not to come close to each till the time we were married.

"It's 10:15 am, we will go out soon", she said.

Till 10:30 am, we sat together on the sofa hiding emotions from each other and what had just happened before 10:15am.

At 10:30 am, we headed out. I was sitting with Katie on the back seat of the car. She busied herself in her laptop, whereas I glued to her extra cell phone. We got lost in our respective worlds. After some time, I got tired. I was leaving no opportunity to sleep and Katie was leaving no opportunity to keep me awake. Sometimes, she poked her pen on my cheek, and sometimes, she touched my hands with her cell phone. Sometimes she spoke on the cell phone.

Katie's car was huge and very comfortable. It was accomodable for a large-sized personality like Katie.

We were glad to return to our normal selves after the dressing room incident. Katie had almost forgotten it.

We had successfully come out of that incident. But, inside of me, I was regretful. I didn't want it to happen. No matter what happens, you can't afford to break anyone's heart. But after all, Katie loved me a lot. The incident can't diminish her love for me, and it remained the same, maybe increased a bit. In fact, it increased gradually. She had really been kind to everything I did.

Finally the car reached the destination. It was an average-sized clinic of high standard but not as good as Katie or Katie's car.

Katie was always there to defend me in all my shyness while consulting the doctor, as she was already aware of my hesitation while interacting with people at such places.

From the moment we entered the clinic till we stepped into the doctor's chamber, everyone was gazing at me. I was feeling very shy and was trying to hide behind Katie who always made me walk beside her. Actually I didn't want to become a centre of attraction, so later when Katie understood my uneasiness she let me walk in the way I wanted to. Katie was acting like a shield for me. Finally, we reached the doctor's cabin. There was a nameplate on the wall with a label of 'Dr. Claudia Lois' on it. Below her name, her degrees were written which attracted me a lot. I imagined my name on place of hers. Katie said, "Come, Cyrus". I followed her. As we entered the cabin, we saw Claudia comfortably sitting on her revolving chair. She was slighting rotating on her chair on its axis. Unlike other doctors, she looked very jovial. She appeared as though she had no interest in her job but enjoys it; unlike others who are working hard just for earning money. She must have a been a jumping jack in her college days. No doubt, these people are extraordinary in their academics and possess great knowledge than their competitors. They look carefree because they believe in enjoying their life to the fullest. They live on the principle of carpe diem which means to make the most of what you have. They can study fifteen to sixteen hours a day and can also work for any given time. They can take any measure, even the wrong path to achieve their aim. Generally, they are very much addicted to vulgarity. They openly express about their intimacy to their friends and also discuss it freely among friends. Claudia was one of such people but with some differences. She was efficient in her skills, but more than that she was a mother to an excellent and talented son. Since her childhood, she had been a brilliant student. In the meantime, she had many bad habits which proved harmful for her in her coming days. She had inherited a great sum of money from her parents. And, her son had multiplied it into more with his skills. He even got monthly salary for this job. But he was never eager to take it. Ultimately, he was the sole gainer. So, why to bother?

Claudia also ran a management institute named after her father. I recalled that there was a big board on the top of the institute which read 'Henry Luis Business School'.

Claudia had a good friend, Lucia Carmel. Lucia was, in fact, her best friend with whom she had completed her higher education. Both of them also shared the similar family story.

Claudia's son was, no doubt, better than Lucia's, so Lucia's son had to assist as a junior 'junior' in terms of both position and profit in the business. Both were quite rich but Claudia always led the command. Lucia was a apparent gentle person, so she never took it to her heart and continued to be with Claudia as a faithful person.

Apparent gentle are the ones who are not truly gentle but lead the life as gentlemen to avoid chaos and unnecessary tension. They are the types who will tolerate your misbehaviour and mischief, but if provoked too much, can be hazardous. Lucia was also like a spoilt college boy but comparatively lesser than Claudia. She had registered her name in almost all the records of wrong deeds. Surprisingly, these two spoilt brats had such talented sons. Their joint effort had taken their management institute to great heights, gaining popularity from everywhere.

We know, bad habits can prove to be dangerous most of the times though may not harm us very few times. Claudia and Lucia also had followed this path. But this time, they had, in front of them, someone who herself was a legend of this path and an apparent gentle person too. And, that person was Katie. So, hopefully, it was going to be a severe clash of their lives.

I guess, it was one of their biggest mistakes to misbehave with me or play with my career. They dared to challenge Katie which was not a wise decision in my opinion. Hence, they had to suffer a great blow and proved to society why indulgence in bad activities is detrimental.

Katie and Claudia wished each other in their own styles, which is hard to understand or even imitate if you are not mature. Maturity at this stage develops a person to face almost any type of situation in his life, whether it is a awkward task or talking to a stranger with confidence. From this age, the misguided person sharpens and polishes his ego. He becomes susceptible of taking any slight mistake of others by heart. He will rarely smile. He will spend most of his time in sadness. The children in the society will wonder why he does not smile or be happy. He will perform his duty with half efficiency. If he gets success, he will express frustration to the world. He will try to put forward that – 'I do hard work and get success. You all lazy fellows are just wasting your time in chatting and roaming'. The success completely gets into his head. Some of them behave kindly while projecting an aura of normalcy despite achieving success. They try to be modest. Sadly, they remain indifferent to the fact that 'being humble' and 'trying to humble' are not the same thing. 'Trying to be humble' attitude removes the pride and arrogance from outside keeping the internal just as before. On the other hand, 'being humble' attitude removes pride and arrogance from outside as well as inside. Such person will never take his success arrogantly. He will always show his concern to others. He'll be polite and kind and will respect everyone. He'll take care of his deeds so that his pain is not inflicted on to others. He will remain tight lipped about his achievements, and will not desire that the people should shower praises on him. This is because, deep inside him, he is already saturated with the appreciations which he gets frequently. Even if you consider that he worked hard for people's appreciations, I'm sure, with a little bit of doubt, that he didn't crave for it. But such person can also become the type of person who tries to be humble, in case he meets continuous failures. During these failures, he gets insulted, troubled and ignored by the people, so he automatically gets driven to the ideas of becoming an egoistic and apparent humble person. It arises, within him, the internal pride which was not in him till he was a real humble person. But in spite of these humiliations, if he keeps his good conduct intact and continues to work hard, he will achieve his success again . . . . which could be even greater than the previous one.

Katie and I sat on the chair. Claudia asked me to sit next to her, on the patient's chair. It was a revolving chair without arms and back-resting part. I began to rotate myself on it. Neither Katie nor Claudia said to me anything for this. I think, they both had been so lost in their discussion that I became a secondary object for them though I was the subject of their discussion. It looked as if they knew each other since many years. In fact, they really did.

I was busy reading the pamphlets kept on the table and the various posters stuck on the walls. I was watching all of them curiously. I wanted to know how it feels like to be a doctor, and that too a renowned one. I also feared that Claudia might scold or shout at me because I was not of her level.

This 'level' gives a person something which we call it as his personality. A doctor or any successful person will have this personality. Even if they travel in a bus, he will behave in the same manner. He'll be what he is. He'll have seriousness in his demeanour. He'll not feel inferior to anybody travelling in a bus as he knows who he is and where he stands in the society. He knows his reality. Even if his co- passenger is wearing a golden watch, he'll not feel intimidated by him. He'll be fine in his silver watch or silver ring. He'll always be satisfied internally and never involve himself in observing what others possess.

I was not a doctor. I was a simple student who neither had eagerness to become a doctor like Claudia nor enough health to earn money by doing physical works. I was a loser on both the ends. In spite of that, I was expecting Carol to marry me who was much ahead of me in all respects. I was having only Katie, who on the contrary, was determined to marry me. again. It was decided that I had to visit the clinic every day. It required some therapy to cure my mental disorder.

Katie introduced me to Claudia as a friend but it was not so easy to fool Claudia who could judge between a friendship and a relation more than a friendship. Katie, too, was not left with any other option.

"Your friend is very beautiful and cute. You're very lucky, Katie, that he is around you for so long. I don't know but you must be feeling very happy when he's around you. Only a brief amount of time has passed since he came here but my mood is refreshed", Claudia expressed. Katie smiled. I wondered how I could be a source of refreshment for Claudia. Claudia further added, "Living far from home, and that too for a twelve-year-old boy, I don't know how he might be managing it". After saying it, she looked at me as though I was awarded a punishment of studies by my home.

"For that, I'm there. He need not worry about that", Katie said without a pause.

"Oh Yes! Katie is there for you, Cyrus. You both are very lucky to have each other. I wished if I was Katie or if Cyrus was my son, I might have been the happiest person of the world", Claudia expressed her desire. I felt as if her excitement was flowing out of her. She was comforting herself by saying such things as she could not come near me.

The vulgar persons are like that only. They know that they can't enjoy with any woman except their wives, so they satisfy their emotions by discussing on sexual topics. Once they start, there's no end to it. They'll give a animalistic smile like that of wolf, crocodile and fox, in between their speech. They'll protest against the vulgarity but still continue to talk about that; it shows their need to cover their vulgar nature. Because If they directly talk on these topics, you will or you can identify their nature but if they will say that these things are harmful you'll be unable to see through their nature. You have no idea about how much enjoyment they can extract from their speech if they are with you. Unfortunately, if a similar kind of person meets them, they might get into a difficult circumstance. But, these people hardly care about that. So, when these two persons sit together, they try to find reasons to stretch their vulgarity. They both will co-operate each other in their vulgar discussion. Even though they both know about each other's intimacy, they will very beautifully hide this fact from each other. They will not see, look or gaze at each girl or woman passing by them. Instead they will stare with their wide open eyes and quench their thirst. After finishing their eye job, they will look at each other and say that the clothes this girl is wearing has become a latest fashion nowadays. Even the girls of my colony have started wearing it. The other one will also agree to this and will add up his comments on this sexual discussion. His comments may also be termed as worthless because he was suddenly distracted from his electrifying thoughts. So, no sensible thing could have come to his mind quickly at that moment. If you ask about the fashion of clothes to a person who was actually seeing more than just clothes, he'll definitely be in a confused state. They both will then try to show that they had forgotten what had just happened. Finally, after a long pause, they'll give their discussion a finishing touch by cursing such things. They will say – 'These things are bad and will push you to the wrong path. Ultimately, you will be in great loss. And, I have taken myself away from these things because I want to lead a peaceful life.'

THE END

This marks the end of a sexual era.

No one may ever know that how many such eras they had already created and ended in their lifetime. Claudia busied Katie in showing pamphlets and other stuffs. Katie was no stranger to this institute, so she was just rolling her eyes casually over those pamphlets and brochures. Meanwhile Claudia called her best friend, Lucia, who was always ready for such stuffs to talk on. If there is any person whom they can use, they would manage even their busiest schedule. Their attitude towards such people is very similar to the thought – 'A fox informed the other fox that it had found a beautiful rabbit. We can have it as a delicious meal'. Such women deserved to be called 'fox' and all other terms denoting disgrace. They were the main causes behind my spoilt career, with Claudia playing the major role, in addition to the initiation.

The wedding ceremony was scheduled to take place at night within a short period of time, so Katie didn't mind waiting for Lucia. I was also busy reading the pamphlets.

It seemed to me a good college. If that was the only college I could go to, for higher studies, I would not have any problem studying in it. Claudia was its chairperson and owner. Her only duty was to take money from the managers which they collected from the students in the form of fee. Lucia was also attached to this institute where she held a respected post for which she got a good amount as salary. It was friendship of Claudia to Lucia that she gave her the golden opportunity to work with her in her own institute, though she was not that promising with regard to her capabilities. The quality I appreciate of this duo was that both took this profession to serve the society. Obviously, they charged money for their treatment but it was very minimal and that too went for charity. The fee structure was prepared in such a way that it could be afforded. The poors were treated free of cost. We see many greedy doctors want innocent people to fall sick or get injured so that they can earn from them. This was not the case with Claudia and Lucia. They chose that profession with a noble thought. Maybe, the success of their institute was a return of that. Remember, people may spend high rate of fees for their education (although education must also be of low cost, especially medical) but when they are ill they pay with a broken heart. And, we should never take advantage of that, especially in the case of the doctors.

Being the only heir of her ancestors, Claudia had boosted her career and reached the success from the money and property left for her by her parents. Annually around five hundred to six hundred students used to look for admission here adding its fund with good amount of fees. So, in this way, Claudia was earning a lot of money from her institution. She could have even slept on the bed made up of currency notes.

Now, to me, she seemed quite successful in her career front. I started to imagine if I would also have created such a successful career in the near future. But Katie was, as usual, normal, because she was habitual to more than these luxuries. Since I was not very possessive of Katie, I was feeling a little inferior to Claudia.

Lucia entered the room. Katie greeted her. Lucia, after looking at me, silently asked Claudia, through the gesture of her eyes, if I was the one for which she had called her. Claudia answered smartly with the same gesture without letting Katie notice it. After Katie, I also wished her in my usual shy manner. Due to my coyness and reserved nature, I could not introduce myself to anybody properly. However, these ladies were experts in understanding a child's feelings and never let me feel shy in their presence.

The three of them talked for some time and then they stood up. Katie asked me to come with her. Katie did not want them to accompany us till the main gate as, without any reason, it would make us a centre of attraction. We wished Claudia and Lucia good luck. Claudia hugged me and kissed me on my cheek. Lucia followed her. I did not like that and Katie was an uneasy observer. She didn't want anyone to come close to me.

Claudia and Lucia tried to cover their acts under the veil of motherly affection. It was not good for these three women to be together anymore. So, we bid each other goodbye and left.

Katie was holding her anger within herself which had aroused due to those two vulgar women. She was grinding her teeth in sheer anger. We quickly went to the car and took our places inside.

Now, Katie started taking out her anger. She was murmuring something. She had a serious look on her face. She had taken that incident on her heart very bitterly. Since she loved me a lot, it was very much obvious that she would get angry.

Claudia and Lucia had taken up a great challenge by teasing the love life of Katie. We have often heard that love is not gentle in all occasions. Sometimes, it takes a fierce turn and become ruthless like lion not allowing anyone to even look at his prey. So it was good not for Claudia and Lucia to do so.

Katie was feeling uncomfortable and restless. She was looking outside the window and was contemplating on something very important. At last, her frustration came out heavily. She said, "Very ill- mannered woman! I don't know how much lust she has". The word 'lust' was strange for me. Even if I was told its meaning, I would not have understood it in the way adults do.

Katie was looking resentful. I asked, "What has happened to you? Why are you looking so angry? And what does this word 'lust' means? You have used it previously also". Katie smiled. Though she tried to control it, the smile came out automatically.

"Nothing . . . . I . . . . I was just angry over their behaviour . . . . kissing you in front of me. It doesn't look good . . . . I mean, it's not the way to see-off anyone . . . . Cyril, if any girl even sees you with a desire or with a different view, I get jealous and annoyed. Claudia and Lucia . . . . I just felt like if they are so eager and interested in kissing, they should go to their private places, call their grandson to them, paint their lips with chocolate and then lick and suck it. That will be enough to satisfy their hunger". Katie could not control her smile and burst into laughter. She was looking pretty in her smiling face with curved and angry eyebrows. You can say that she was looking like a clever and naughty child. The word 'chocolate' in her angry speech reminded me of the chocolate which used to appear in the television commercial. It was a 'Hershey' chocolate. The Hershey Company had launched that variety of chocolate which felt very soft and melting in the mouth.

In that very commercial, everyone was eating it in a very strange manner. They were enjoying its sticky and melting flavour. They were licking their fingers and the chocolate got spread all around their lips and cheeks. I yearned for the newly launched Hershey chocolate. I wanted to eat it, and that too in the same manner in which the children in the commercial were eating it.

I had also challenged my friends that I could eat that chocolate without licking. It was not easy or you can say that it was impossible because as soon as you start unwrapping the inner cover, it would start showing its true colours. It was proved that it can be eaten only in the way shown in the commercial.

It was the right time to buy that because my motherly girlfriend, Katie, was with me. Katie used to give me everything even before I could ask her for it. So there was no point that she would deny my idea. I had one advantage with Katie that I didn't have to persuade her for anything like small kids do for buying something. She was like a mother who would fulfil all the wishes of her child . . . . a mother to whom the society refers to as the spoiler of her child. But, I was very disciplined and never took due-advantage of Katie. My moral values and polite behaviour always held importance for me in my life. And, I think, this had added to my beauty. I was always well behaved and polite towards Katie and never misused her feelings of love for any kind of mischief.

I was resting on the super-comfortable seat of the car, whereas Katie was constantly rotating a pen in her hand. She was lost in some thoughts. She was quiet because she didn't want to disturb me. She knew that I was very tired.

Being physically weak, I always felt tired and looked for comfort, rest and sleep. I was fussy in the matters of my intakes. Maybe, this was the reason for my poor health. And, after the entry of such a lenient person, Katie, into my life, my health was sure to deteriorate. It was a great challenge for Katie to improve my health and at the same time keep me happy. It's because making me upset would break her heart, on the other side, falling down of my health would become a concern for her.

Perhaps there were no chances of further downfall of my health and I being alive at the same time because I was already on the edge of dying. I was on the lowest level of health. Any further reduction would have paved my way to death. I was never worried about my health but it was a matter of great disturbance for Katie. Hence, sometimes, a little sign of tension was apparently viewed on her face. Though she always maintained her composure but becoming a perfect person was impossible for her.

"Katie", I said, as she came out of her deep thought. I started smiling and felt shy. She understood that I wanted something but was feeling shy to voice it.

"What, Cyril?", she asked, as she looked at me with a smile.

"I want chocolate. The one that comes in the television commercial", I said in a shy tone which appeared very innocent to Katie. She asked her driver to buy some for me.

Till the time he brought the chocolates, I kept smiling for Katie but as soon as it came in my hands, I, along with it, got lost in my own world.

Till we were married, Katie didn't touch me and maintained that behaviour patiently. And, I liked that. Maybe, Katie herself would have been surprised at such level of patience in her. I hardly put a check on her after the auditorium incidence.

This behaviour of mine, of asking for the chocolate, was not justified. I was behaving very selfishly with Katie. For asking for any help, I went to Katie and she would very willingly help me. But, as soon as my motive was fulfilled, I used to get lost in the thoughts of Carol. That was the time I should have spent with Katie. It was a selfish behaviour which I was showing to Katie and she was patiently tolerating it. Perhaps, it was Katie's immense love for me which gave her the power to bear a childish, reserved and selfish person like me.

When you have love for someone, you will ignore all his negative traits and will give reasons for that negativity just in order to favour him and support him in every way possible.

While playing game on her cell phone, I had fallen asleep in the car. When we reached the house, the servants took me to the bed. I found myself on bed, when I opened my eyes. I saw Katie studying on her table. In spite of being so busy carrying the responsibilities, she had not lost her sincerity for her studies. It impressed me very much. Some parents and teachers tell their students and kids, "You look good while studying and bad while playing". This saying was appearing to be true this time. Katie was looking beautiful when she was studying. In fact, it was her sincerity that had added to her beauty.

I stretched myself in laziness. I picked up the chocolates that were kept on the table beside me and again got lost in that. When I got my eyes off the chocolates, I looked at Katie. She gave me a very warm smile.

This smile always comforted me. This smile is what a person wants when he wakes up from his sleep but usually never gets it. When he wakes up after sleeping post the lunch, the persons around him show their dull faces indicating that they are angry with him because he had wasted his time in sleeping. Sleeping after the sunrise is a wasteful thing but the post-lunch sleep of around an hour is good for health. It refreshes us to perform the further activities of the day properly.

Katie had a unique affection and attitude towards me loving me in every way and in every possible

manner. It felt as if I had got a person who'll love me, care for me, and be with me forever, as a well- wisher. If only I would have realised her importance and the importance of her love, I would not have faced the worst time of my life that is being on the verge of suicide. But I think it would not have been a justice that I would not bear the pain in spite of breaking Katie's heart all the time. It's unfair that the person who hurts another person every now and then (and that too the one who loves him so dearly) would not be penalised.

I stood up but then sat down on the bed due to my laziness.

"Are you doing your homework?", I asked.

"No, I'm completing the chapter that I had planned in my schedule", Katie replied.

"Have you completed the homework already?", I asked in a surprised tone.

"Yes", came the reply from Katie in a very humble tone.

I used all my strength to reach to Katie and sat beside her. She started talking to me so that I may not feel ignored, but I could see that it was affecting her studies and schedule. So, I told her to continue her study and added, "I won't speak till you study. Till then I'll play games on the cell phone".

I never studied with my own interest because I knew that at some time during the whole day Katie will make me study. She would make me finish my homework and explain the whole chapter to me. So, why should I bother when Katie had taken the responsibility of my studies and me too?

Till about forty-five minutes, there was a complete silence. I was also trying my best to make the environment congenial for Katie. I was playing games keeping its sound on mute.

After completing her work, Katie kept her books aside and began to talk. Since we were going to marry that night, Katie was talking about academics just to increase the affection caused due to physical and mental detachment of romance between us. In addition to that, I, being a career-oriented person, was interested in those talks of academics.

For me, that marriage was of no happiness. I did not understand the depth of the marriage nor the liabilities it imposes on one. In fact, I was not mature enough to take that marriage seriously. For me, it was just an extended form of friendship.

I only knew that a boy and girl are not allowed to touch each other before marriage. They should not even talk romantically. Forget about sex. In fact, I did not know what 'sex' meant. The only access I had to this term 'sex' was through application forms or sometimes in the newspaper. It was not a word which would bring a naughty smile to my face though everyone in my class laughed and smiled at the mere pronunciation of that. I had no idea about the human reproductive system. I didn't even know that in order to have a child, the couple has to do something which is made a laughing and giggling matter by the people of our society.

I still remember one incident of my class in the coaching institute. The number of boys was equal to the number of girls in the class. Boys called it a perfect ratio as one girl could be paired with one boy. I was junior to almost all the boys and girls. Fifteen years was the average age in our class, though some were too old for that stage of education. After all, who knows the correct age? But, in my case, I was truly twelve-year-old tiny person. Boys enjoyed with my innocence and girls also left no opportunity. Boys always used to talk about intimate things. Even the girls were no less in this field. Their sole aim behind this was to show that they were grown-ups. In reality, they couldn't do that, so they used to extract pleasure by doing that verbally. They never studied and had no aim of what they have to study on a particular day. Except a few, all of them seemed to be of that category. Discussion about men and women were no unusual topic for them, but there was one person about whom they often talked. That person was the receptionist of the coaching institute. They considered that woman very beautiful. They always found some or the other reason to talk to her. Not only they, but everyone in the institute pursued her. And, I think she had no problem with it. She might have done that high level make-up of her face till the world accepted her as beautiful.

When a woman observes that the people around her are looking at her . . . . admiring her beauty . . . . she has become a centre of attraction and a topic of discussion, she feels elated within. Never think that she feels uncomfortable at this rather she feels as one of the happiest persons on earth. Only a girl with high values and a firm belief system would take it as abnormal as she has got the moral values instilled into her and knows the most appropriate way in which a girl should behave. The receptionist of the coaching institute was without a doubt a disciplined and moralistic woman but there was some sort of pretentious nature in her. I think, she should have focused more on her duty.

It's not bad to beautify yourself but one shouldn't neglect his responsibility. In fact, work should get one of the topmost priority in your list. If you are excellent in your job, it will add to your beauty and people will respect you for that.

I always hesitated while speaking to any stranger. So, with the receptionist, it became too difficult for me to talk. Moreover, since I was not old enough, there was no room for enjoyment for me. I think, she would have been upset that I was not attracted to her whereas the other boys in my class used to crave for her. But she might not have been surprised much. She knew that I was only twelve years old.

They had come with a goal of becoming successful engineers and what they were up to in reality! All these used to upset me a lot.

A boy among them said, "When I heard that the receptionist had become mother of a child, I got shattered. I could not sleep that night . . . . You don't know how much I love her".

I thought, "She was not fortunate enough to have a husband before she gave birth to a child. It's so sad she became mother before getting married. That's why people are worried to get their daughter married at the appropriate age so that their daughter doesn't get pregnant before the marriage".

A woman becoming pregnant was a miracle to me. Previously, I thought that girls never wanted this miracle to happen before their marriage. I didn't even know that this miracle happens only after marriage and sometimes its absence can cause divorce between a happy couple. "Is she married?", I asked. My face was shining with the polish of surprise as well as innocence.

After this something that I class burst into an question of mine, I had to face can't describe in words. The whole uncontrollable laughter.

My question had become a source of enjoyment for the whole class; both boys and girls enjoyed to their fullest.

I hope nobody in the class who witnessed it can ever forget the incident, which in return taught me a lesson of not to speak anything in the class unnecessarily.

"It's like a dream come true for me, Cyril. You can't even imagine how much happy I am", Katie said. She was looking like a kid whose face shines after getting a box full of toffees.

We got married at night as per my preference and in the way I wanted it to be. The marriage was solemnised successfully the way we wanted including all the other things arrangements.

I was wearing black suit, whereas Katie was in a sober beautiful dark brown gown. Both of our dresses were simple.

I got tired by the end of the marriage.

"Not many people marry at the same day as their birthday. You are a lucky one, Cyril", Katie said. I smiled and got busy in the flowers that we got during the marriage ceremony. Katie said further, "Only fifteen minutes more and you'll turn a year older. After fifteen minutes, the New Year is going to arrive.

We'll celebrate both your birthday and the New Year in the presence of close friends and my family members. You feel uncomfortable? I know that you have hesitation amidst many guests. Isn't it, Cyril?"

I smiled and nodded.

"I want to change my dress. I want to wear my night dress. This suite is not comfortable at this time. I want to lie down comfortably on the bed", I said.

Katie replied, "Yes, I'm bringing it". She slightly smiled at this as she walked towards the wardrobe to bring my dress.

The dark blue colour sweatshirt and black trouser she brought for me. It was one of my favourites.

"I should also change. I'll give you company in the nightdress", Katie said. She went to the wardrobe again.

She returned to me and then sat beside me with a bundle of clothes. "Cyril, I know your choices and also the colours you like. But today it's a very special occasion and I want you to select among these.

Please tell me, Cyril, which one should I wear tonight?". I had a small list of likes. I searched through uncountable dresses she brought one after the other. After sometime, I stopped her from bringing any more as it was a heap of clothes in front me. At the back of my head, I was wondering about price value of those clothes. Honestly, there were too many. Finally, I selected five pairs. All the trousers I selected were of black colour. The sweatshirts I selected were of dark blue, dark red, dark green, dark brown and dark black colours, respectively. But I could not choose one among these. The problem was not that I couldn't pick up my favourite one. I would have easily gone for the dark-brown colour but I couldn't refuse the rest of that. I wanted to see Katie in all those dresses. I knew she would look gorgeous in the brown one but others too were very attractive.

It was really hard for me to select only one. So I needed Katie's help. I told her what was going on in my mind. Katie, as per expectations, gave a heart-melting reply, "Okay! There's no problem. I'll wear all the five one by one during the night. Lastly, I'll wear the brown one. I want you to fall asleep very peacefully, and, I think, this brown dress will be very helpful in that. I want that moment to be imprinted on your memory forever". She impressed me immensely by her statement. I could not imagine how much she loved me. Even in the matter of choosing a perfect dress, she left no opportunity to please me. She had proved that she was the person who loved me the most (in terms of both quantity and quality).

My birthday was celebrated at night as per my request and the way I wanted it to happen. Only Katie, Katie's family and I were the ones who were the part of that celebration. After that, the new year was celebrated on the behest of my childish innocence. Nobody wished to remain awake for late hours to celebrate the New Year.

Certainly, it was the best birthday and New Year celebration of my life. All the things I demanded were included in that celebration. Every person, that is, Katie and Katie's family, seemed to be enjoying to the fullest. There was no tension of the expense it was going to cost. And why that would be? After all, they were the persons whom people called as 'sophisticates'. I had celebrated my birthdays before too but it was exclusive. If the previous birthday celebrations would have been so expensive, sadness would have been prevailed all over the faces, which could spoil the mood of the party. Afterwards, I would think that it would have been better if there was not such a lavish celebration.

Now everything was over or it can also be said that a new celebration was about to start.......... a celebration which was private . . . . only Katie's voice could be heard . . . . and that too whispers coming out as a result of long separation between me and her.

Katie and I had changed our clothes. We were in our pre-decided night dresses, that is, sweatshirt and cotton trouser.

I was feeling very relieved after taking off the wedding suit. I was lying on the bed. I was completely peaceful in my mind. Though there was sadness in me at the death of Alfredo's family members but Katie's words of consolation had immensely helped me to come back to my normal mental status which I had lost.

Being an orphan, Alfredo and his family were the only ones whom I could call as mine. I was brought up in Alfredo's house. Alfredo and I grew up together. So, I always considered Alfredo and his family members as my own family.

Neither Alfredo nor I was responsible for this misery. But, you can say that Alfredo himself knitted the cause of their death.

Alfredo's presence in my life made Claudia and Lucia uncomfortable. Alfredo was the hurdle in their ways to reach me. So, a well-organised plan was made to teach him a lifelong lesson. Moreover, Katie and I could also be separated. What more could they ask for?

It was Claudia who was the master mind behind the whole strategy. But, when I came to know the reality, it was already too late. From some sources close to Katie's family, I got to know that Claudia knew me before we met her. Katie had often discussed about me with her. Since Katie was too happy to have me as a friend, she had poured a little bit of this happiness to her friend, Claudia.

In spite of the vast age difference between them, they were good friends of each other, which I admire but I was surprised as Claudia was not worth it. Katie always respected Claudia but Claudia never accepted her reverence ever. I think she didn't deserve it.

Katie had shown some of my photographs to Claudia in her mobile. Some of those had me and Katie together in a smiling pose. At that time only, Claudia decided to snatch me from Katie. Such was her jealousy towards our beautiful relationship. She had made up her mind that she would have me in her life completely. No sharing with Lucia. If she can't get me, it can be tolerated but Katie's or anyone else's presence in my life irritated her. So, Claudia, out of her jealousy, made some video clips in which Alfredo was in a drunken state. Some photographs were also clicked. And, these were sent straight to his family. The rest you can imagine yourself.

The response from his family members was beyond expectations. I think, the family members were shocked at Alfredo's deeds who was guilt-ridden. They could have tolerated if it was me in place of him because I was tagged as immature. But, Alfredo in such a state . . . . it was quite astonishing for them. Alfredo was considered an example of sincerity and obedience. He was so obedient that sometimes the word 'obedient' seemed small for him.

Everyone in home saw video clips and photographs sent by Claudia and were deeply hurt. Claudia did this to ruin my relationship with Katie. Claudia didn't know that Alfredo's family was a bit different in this case. She didn't know that after seeing these photographs and video clips, they will react in a totally strange manner. They will not investigate into the matter. They will not search for the truth. They will just sit with their dropped faces and mourn. Father will be sad. Cousins will be sadder. And, mother will be the saddest. Father and cousins will ponder upon any positivity and take this case to their brains, whereas mother will take that straight to her heart. The more you'll console her, the more disheartened she'll become. Then, everyone will think of any idea to comfort her. And, the very idea of comforting her became the first step towards their death. It happened when everyone decided to take mother somewhere for an outing. It was somewhere in the city itself. So, in the journey, in the process of comforting, the cousin, who was driving the car, lost his concentration and along with others breathed his last. When I was told about this, I was heartbroken. No one, except Katie, was able to console me.

Now, I realized what went wrong while I was sleeping, or more appropriately, unconscious, in Claudia's house.

Claudia had invited Katie for the birthday party of her grandson. She had especially told Katie to bring me along with her. I was shown the PlayStation and the other things which attracted me. During the party, I requested Katie to wait for some more time because I was nearing the end of a game on the PlayStation. Also, the games in Claudia's house were different than that of Katie's, and I was shy of asking Katie for that.

Through some people, I came to know that Alfredo was given a glass of juice with some medicines mixed in it to make him unconscious. It was given when I was busy playing games with other children present there. And, after that, the main part of the plan was executed.

Claudia knew that I was a game addict so she used my addiction as her weapon. She also made some children wait after the party so that Katie might not get suspicious about her intentions.

I was shocked when I was informed that just to destroy my relationship with Katie, Claudia went to such an extent of her criminal thoughts.

Claudia and Lucia had done their job, and now it was their turn to taste the flavour of pain. You'll be surprised to know that they both were murdered, and even more surprised that the murderer of these two was no one but they themselves.

Claudia had gone to Lucia's house with the intention of killing her. She had planned to shoot Lucia with her gun. She had told Lucia that she wanted to discuss some business plans with her. Lucia didn't know about her cruel intentions. Lucia thought that Claudia was still a friend to her. Claudia had expressed herself so nicely that no one might had found out what she was up to . . . . not even Lucia. On the other hand, Lucia was no less than Claudia. She had also planned the same. She had also expressed herself very nicely. They both were unaware of each other's intentions.

It is worth noting that I was the cause of the death of Alfredo's family members and I only became the cause of the death of these two women. It's true that they did not intend to take the lives of Alfredo's family members but, yes, they had surely sewn the circumstances for that. My position in their life was ironical. I gave them all sorts of happiness and at the same time I only became the reason of their destruction.

Claudia was suspicious about Lucia's fidelity and was fearful regarding their crime to come out in the world. Lucia was also entertaining the same thought against Claudia. But both were unaware of one another's selfish motives. I was their main focus of interest. A clash was there on the horizon, as I could not be divided into two equal halves like a cartoon. It needed their co-operation and compromise hand to hand in order to avoid conflict. But, both the ladies lack such qualities in their characters.

The news of their death was a sudden shock for everyone.

Claudia visited Lucia's house. After chatting for a few minute, she went straight to act upon her decision for what she had come.

Lucia was dead on one single shot. But, even Claudia couldn't remain free from her own sin. She fell on the ground. After some time, she also left the world because she had drunk the glass of juice in which the poison was mixed. Lucia had poisoned only one of the two glasses. Claudia, after killing Lucia, developed an urge(which is natural) of drinking both the glasses. And so, you can say that, with the ending of that urge, ended the life of Claudia. Both the women faced a terrible death. But, surely suicide is a more terrible death than that.

"Hey, Cyril!", Katie interrupted my thought just at the right time. I called it the 'right time' because I was finished with one thought and some other thoughts were about to invade my mind.

Katie smiled and came close to me. She laid beside me keeping the upper part of her body not in contact with the bed. She rested herself on her elbow in a straight position. Her legs were lying on the bed and the elbow was slightly at a distance from my head.

We got lost into our own world. She was caressing my forehead and hairs. She was happy which was clearly visible on her face. But, it can't be measured.

She sided the hairs scattered on my forehead and then kissed my forehead. She also kissed the hair which was a bit weird for me. I mean to say – Are the hairs also the things for kissing? Before meeting her, I didn't know that when you are married to someone who loves you a lot, and if you're lying with him on the bed, then he will like you to such an unknown extent that even your eyes, eyebrows, chin and ears will attract them. You just can't stop that person because they care for you a lot. The same was with me and Katie.

After kissing my forehead, Katie gazed into my eyes, at eyebrows, ears, chin, neck and cheeks. She didn't kiss them. She just touched them with her fingers. And at last, she enclosed me in her arms like a mother does with her child. I think, she was shy to land on the lips. And, more than her, I was hesitant. She knew that I would have felt shy if she did that. So, she limited her satisfaction. But, I think, that's not how a married couple feels. Everyone feels shy but not as much as I was. Those kisses of Katie were not something which could make someone laugh or intimate mentally. It's just the emotion which was coming out. It's just a sign of love . . . . a symbol of love . . . . and every husband and wife might be doing this. This is what a husband and wife expect from each other. You should also think that if love is overflowing from Katie, then what would she do next? You'll guess that she must have hugged me. But if that's not proving to be enough, then what should she do now? Should she tear up the pillow? Should she start throwing the chair? Should she start throwing her dresses or should she punch the wall? All these things are not good and will only harm her. Here, if a kiss can normalise her, then what's the problem? Calling her sexual or intimate would be wrong, if just a kiss can satisfy her heart and mind romantically. After all, she was my wife and was just kissing her husband and not to any stranger. So, she was right in all respects. Here, she kissed her husband and her kiss in the auditorium was to a stranger which had a very huge difference. The latter one was immoral, whereas the former one was her right. Katie was constantly looking into my eyes. Since she was unstoppable, I too gave her tough competition. I was acting childish as there was rigidity in my way of looking into her eyes but she was truly lost in me.

Finally when she appeared hard to defeat, I interrupted her. "Why are you constantly looking at me?", I asked.

Her reply was a heart melting one. She said, "I'm not looking you. I'm just looking myself in your eyes". She smiled and further added, "First, I saw you as a whole. Then, I started seeing your face, then eyes and then into your eyes. I was ensuring my presence in your eyes. If I could see my whole image in your eyes, then it will be confirmed that you too are looking into my eyes . . . . you too are lost in me . . . . but I think, you were also looking in the same manner at me why?". She was wearing a naughty smile on her face.

"I was just giving you a tough competition", I replied. Her smile became more shining. She pulled my cheek and could not resist smiling further. She brought her face close to mine and expressed the deep feelings caged into her heart. In a soft low voice, she said,

"Cyril . . . . you're looking very beautiful . . . . charming . . . . Cyril, you're glowing". She continued, "You're eyes are very beautiful . . . . you're lips are very beautiful . . . . you are so beautiful". I was overwhelmed with joy listening to her words and also knowing that there was someone in this world who loved me.

We both talked for a while. It was a very pleasant moment for both of us. It was a moment to enjoy each other's presence in tranquility a moment for which people strive in life.

This time, my interaction with Katie made me a mature person in just a few minute. I also started talking like a grown-up man. But, it could not be continued for long because you can't expect a young teenager to completely behave like an adult.

Katie had, one by one, tried all the chosen outfits except that brown sweatshirt and black trouser.

Finally, she came dressed up in the brown sweatshirt and black trouser. I was pleased to see her in that dress. By that time, I was feeling very sleepy and Katie had also noticed that. Then, like a kid sleeps with his mother, l slept enclosed in Katie's arms.

Obviously, we didn't have sex, and you know why.

Katie would not have asked for more. Her dream boy was so close to her.

After marriage, Katie and I shifted to New York. And, Alfredo always kept that secret to himself, hidden from everyone around him.

We both were very happy in each other's company. Katie supported me in everything I aspired to be and wanted to do, which was always very firmly rooted into my moral belief system. She gave everything I ever wanted to have. But, in spite of her unwavering love and devotion for me, it was surprising that I still wanted to end my life.

ON THE VERGE OF SUICIDE

WHAT I THINK is that we are never alone. Even if we have none to talk to us, we start talking to ourselves. In fact, we talk to ourselves more than to anyone, in our lifetime. What is going on in our mind is kept hidden from the world. We reveal or speak only selected words to anyone, despite having many more thoughts. The rest wanders in our minds which listen to these things very carefully.

But, the thing which should be noticed is that, in spite of using selected words in front of others, a dispute may occur. Imagine what would be the outcome if whatever we think takes shape of words and is disclosed to the world.

Some people are reserved. We say that they talk very less. We are right here. But there is something valuable to be added to this. These persons have got a very active brain which is always going through some debates. Among them, there is a group which is very far ahead. This group is hanging between life and death. We generally consider money, hiding truth, family and other things as our reason to get worried. But, the people of this group have crossed that mental state. They directly plunge into the matter of life and death. These people are the ones who want to commit suicide. No matter how much you try to moralise them, they are stubborn and remain that way only, being more and more demoralised. They will always search for the opportunity to kill themselves. Negative thoughts will keep hovering around them. Even if the positive thoughts come to their minds, they will ignore them. 'Depressed' is the most common word to describe them.

The first love is usually very memorable and can't be forgotten. The name of Carol, who was my first and the only love, was carved in my mind very deeply. The relationship with Katie was still not the one which could be called as love. She, in a haste and excitement, made me agree to her marry her. She tried to induce love in me for her but it was just a temporary one. Therefore, everything was like a diluted solution. And, it's not surprising that Katie knew all that. A girl like Katie could detect from your face what you are most probably up to or maybe she was intuitive enough to read the signs correctly. She knew that I did not feel free in her house. She knew that Carol's name was deeply imprinted on my mind and it was not so easy to erase that word.

When you are not fully committed in love with a person, you are not completely into him. You will talk to that person with only half of your concentration. You will try to get off him very quickly. You will talk to him just as a formality. Whenever that person comes to you, your heart becomes somewhat reluctant to acknowledge that. Sometimes, it may become the cause of your rudeness to him.

I was experiencing the same, with Katie. I had married a person whom I didn't love. Though Katie convinced me to marry her but I didn't know why I was never attracted to her. No matter how much she hugged me, I didn't feel the joy of love. It's true that a young teenager may not feel the pleasure of a hug as much as an adult but at least he will feel the pleasure of the friendship. But, unfortunately, I couldn't feel even that for her.

I had realised that you should marry a person who loves you and also whom you love. I'm not criticising the system of arranged marriage, the age-old tradition of many countries. I'm talking about those who believe in love marriage and are looking forward to spend their whole life with someone whom they love. But my suggestion for the previous one is that the parents should never deprive their children from participating in this decision with the full rights.

My marriage couldn't be categorised into love or arranged. I don't know what it should be called.

Now, since I was still away from the love of my life, I was slowly moving towards a dangerous destination. It is one of the worst things in this world.

You don't commit suicide at once. Instead, you slowly prepare yourself for it and that too because of yourself. Perhaps, sometimes others push you towards it, but as you know, whether you or the other is the cause of it, a suicide is a suicide only which kills you and none else. A suicide committed because of others will not be called a murder neither it will be turned it into a courageous act from a coward's deed. The world will mock you and will have no respect for you. If you commit suicide because of others, do you know what will they say about you among themselves? They'll say, "He was such a duffer to give up before us. We were so strong that we made him sacrifice his life for us". Ask yourself—'Were you such a weak and stubborn person to sacrifice yourself for them? Was the value of your life so little that you sacrificed it for them?' In the whole matter, you'll be the sole sufferer; you lost your life. The world will remember you as a person who led a sad life and ended it in one of the saddest way.

Suppose, if a group of people ask you to sacrifice your life so that they could become rich. You will obviously neglect it. You will accept the death given to you while trying to save your life but you won't sacrifice your life for them. It means that you will make efforts to come out of your difficulty rather than kneeling down in front of them and asking them to behead you. If you would have done it at that place, then why not here? Why did you kneel down before these people? How can these people persuade you to commit suicide? How can you become a puppet in their hands? Instead, you should stand up for yourself and fight away. And, such attitude deserves a salute. Once you start fearing, they'll scare you more and more. And, then, you'll be like a remote-controlled toy car at their fingertips.

There are innumerable reasons to enjoy the life if you start having a positive attitude. We have got the life to live, make and build. No matter how small the life is, make it appear big. But, the person who is about to commit suicide usually pays a deaf ear to such reality. If only he listens to it carefully and obliges to take it to his heart, he'll be saved from a dangerous crime. This person should simply remember and follow one thing – "I will just not commit suicide". He should say in his mind – "I'll do anything. I'll jog or roll on the ground.

I'll run, punch the table, roam around or do anything useless or crimeless but I'll not commit suicide. I'll carry my life forward in every way possible. I'll lead a simple life with a simple house, simple food and simple living style but I'll carry my life forward. And, when death will come to me by itself, I'll happily embrace it".

When a child does not eat food, his parents make him understand the nutritional value of food and advise him to have it in order to grow stronger. He, then obeys them without questioning any further. It continues for for several years and then a time comes when he becomes a full grown healthy man. For that child, the benefit of eating the food was unknown but after several years he realises that.

Similarly, when a person, who is about to commit suicide, is told not to do it, and he obeys, his weakness will turn into his strength and he'll get ready to lead his life normally. But the problem is that he is unknown just like that child.

When a child falls ill and refuses to eat the bitter medicine, his parents persuade him to take it. He, then obeys them without questioning any further. It continues for a few days and then a day comes when he's cured of his ailment. For that child, the benefit of eating the bitter medicine was unknown but after a few days he realises that. Similarly, when a person, who is about to commit suicide, is told not to commit it, and he obeys, his sick life will also be cured like that of the sick child. But, the problem is that he is unknown just like that sick child.

When a person gets hurt and a wound appears on his body, he visits the doctor. The doctor does the dressing and applies some medicinal paste on it. The person cries because of the chilled sensation of the paste and sometimes shakes himself as a result of the pain. He may ask the doctor to apply some other less painful paste but the doctor doesn't listen to him and tells him to get that particular paste only. He suggests the person that it will benefit him. The patient, then obeys without questioning any further. It continues for a few minute(and a few days after this) and then a day comes when his wound heals. For that patients, the benefit of the medicinal paste was unknown but after a few days he realises that. Similarly, when a person, who is about to commit suicide, is told not to commit it, and he obeys, his wounded life will also be healed like that of the wound of the person. But, the problem is that he is unknown just like that patient.

When a student, sitting in a mathematics class, complains that he is unable to understand the concept, the teacher advises him to first pay attention to the lecture patiently. The teacher says – "First, listen to my whole lecture. Your confusion will get vanished". The student, then obeys without questioning any further. It continues for a few minute and then a time come when his confusion is removed. For that student, the benefit of listening to the whole lecture of his teacher was unknown but after a few minute he realises that. Similarly, when a person, who is about to commit suicide, is told not to commit it, and he obeys, his confusion between suicide and living the life will be removed like that of the student. But, the problem is that he is unknown just like that student.

When a person wants to open a roadside restaurant and also longs to have a lot of fruit trees in his orchard, he will go to an expert of that field. Now, when that expert helps and guides him, he will question

– *"Why is this particular process followed in the cooking? Why not the other? Why is this particular process followed in farming? Why not the other?".* *Then, the expert will suggest him to follow only those processes and will add that only those processes are suitable and beneficial. The businessman, then obeys without questioning any further. It continues for a few months or years and a day comes when his dreams takes its shape and he establishes himself as the owner of a renowned restaurant. His orchard gets filled with juicy fruits. For that businesses, the benefit of following those particular processes was unknown but after a few months or years he realises that. Similarly, when a person, who is about to commit suicide, is told not to commit it, and he obeys, his penniless and drought-like- appearing life will also become poverty-less and joyful. But, the problem is that he is unknown . . . . just like that businessman.*

So, a person, who is about to commit suicide, should say to himself— "I'll carry my life forward . . . . I'll live . . . . I'll live and I'll live". He should say to himself –

"The child, who used to refuse the food, is similar to my problem. That food seemed like a burden to him. Similarly, life, which is looking burdensome to me, will no longer be a burden for me. Life may have some burden-like difficulties but I'll carry these burden-like situations of life and I hope that a strong and healthy life will welcome me very soon. The child, who used to refuse to eat the bitter medicine, is similar to my problem. Life may also have some bitterness like that of medicine but I'll drink that bitter situation of life. And, I hope that a cured bright life will come very soon. The patient, who was requesting the doctor to apply some other medicinal paste on his wound, is similar to my problem. Life may also have some painful experiences but I'll take all those pain, and I'm sure that a healed life will come to me very soon. The student, who was unable to understand the concept in mathematics, is similar to me. Life may also have confusion between committing suicide and living but I'll quietly pass by these confusions and I hope that a peaceful life will come very soon. The person, who was worried about the processes being followed in his restaurant and orchard, is similar to my problem. Life may also have situations in which we may become impatient but I'll work hard and wait for the right time and I hope that a poverty-less and tasteful life will come very soon".

A hard-working person enjoys his life in a way you may never know or imagine. He'll always be content with whatever he possesses. He'll have a satisfied heart and calm mind, but you cannot figure it out by merely seeing at his face. Still, he'll look thousand times better than the gloomy and mourning person who is always idle and does nothing. And, when that negative person is up to with something, it is suicide which is one of the worst things in the world.

Your life is like a book. It has happiness written in it. Life, in reality, is a very precious gift to us. It's you who make it terrible. Life, in reality, is full of happiness but sometimes sadness too comes to pay a visit. Ignorant and weak people take this sadness to their heart and eventually commit suicide. They don't dare to turn the page of their life's book. They don't know, that, on the next page, happiness is written. They can't bear the sadness, and, out of depression, they commit suicide. Had they turned the next page, they would have enjoyed happiness. But, they are already riding the horse of impatience which ultimately brings them to the valley of suicide. The horse of impatience saves itself in this process and then rides back to find out other depressed weakling.

So, at least turn the sad page of your life's book even if the sad page comes in front of your eyes. Happiness may be written on the very next page. What you have to do is turn over the page.

I was married to Katie, a person who loved me the most among all people in my life(I mean to say that nobody loved me more than Katie). Also, among others, I was the one whom Katie loved the most. These two sentences bring out very different meanings, if you think over it deeply.

I was having a wife for whom every person would have craved for. I was having everything I desired or anyone might desire. In spite of all that, I wanted to put an end to my life. Anyone would have been puzzled to know that. Even I was surprised, sometimes. And, it was very late when I realised that the cause of this feeling of suicide was one and only person, Carol.

I didn't know what golden characteristic Carol had that attracted me to her more than Katie. I mean, she was not so beautiful, not so good in behaviour towards me and not so good in studies. I didn't know what compelled me to praise her in front of everyone and even in front of Katie. Imagine, how much Katie's heart would have wept at that.

I wasted the golden years of my teenage life for Carol. I wasted my career for her . . . . wasted myself for her which was above everything else. And, on the other hand, Katie wasted herself for me.

Fortunately, Katie got selected in Harvard and her performance was also jaw-dropping and much more brilliant than that of anyone. But, she couldn't replace my role models, David and Billy. Also, I considered them better than Katie in spite of knowing that they were not. Neither David nor Billy might have ever matched Katie's brilliance; still I praised both of them more than Katie. I think, the reason behind this was my dislike towards her . . . . I didn't like her company. I think her over—expressive and forceful love irritated me always being too caring about me, telling me what to do and what not to do at every step as if I was a brainless person. She was too possessive and too protective about me. Firstly, I didn't like her and didn't love her. And, over and above that, she always showed her over-expressive love to me.

But, if Carol would have loved me like that, I would have been happy to a great degree.

Spending days sitting idle, failing in every examination and hating Katie had become a usual routine for me. For the whole day, in spite of being with Katie, I used to think about Carol. I expected her to begin loving me some day. Carol was in U.S. for a short time for pursuing higher education. But, I heard that she returned to Milan due to financial troubles.

Even if I spotted Carol passing by me on the streets of New York, I felt refreshed. On thinking about her, my heartbeat always skipped a beat. And, I think, it is one of the first signs of your love towards a female person. During my study time, I always turned my eyes away from the book after only a few second. Then, I would start thinking about Carol. Her image used to flash in front of my eyes. Moreover, the mental problem, which was on its peak, added fuel to the fire. And, I think, that mental problem alone could single-handedly push me to commit suicide.

Neither was I getting academic success nor was I able to get Carol's love in my life. The days seemed mundane and gloomy to me and the arrival of Katie made it even worse. And Katie, on the contrary, felt refreshed and happier after meeting me.

Katie knew that I didn't like her company so she used to be with me only for a short period of time, though the meeting occurred a number of times during the day. She might have been aware of all these things cropping up in my head. But, certainly, she might not have ever thought about my decision to commit suicide. In addition, she might not have known that it was Carol who was indirectly the sole reason behind my decision to commit suicide.

Carol, on the other hand, would not have even bothered about my feelings for her. It would be obviously not going to affect her that how much I loved her. The reality was that I was of no importance to Carol of no use for her. I should have understood this earlier. Avoiding to recognise me if we passed by each other, maintaining a distance from me, staring at me as if I had a fight with her. Those were the signs which indicated her hatred for me forget about the word 'not loving'.

If a person does not love you, it's comparatively a better situation than the hatred. You just have to make him love you. But, if a person hates you and you want him to love you, then it's a doubled-up job. You have to first make him stop hating you. Then, you have to strive hard to induce love in him, for you. So, you have to increase your efforts here.

These sorts of philosophical thoughts used to pop up in my mind.

A person, who is depressed with his life, has got only these things to ponder upon. He spends the major part of his day thinking about such things. Sometimes, in front of the people, when he speaks about these thoughts, they suggest him not to think much and focus on the work. The people are absolutely right in this case. But it can't make any difference in the life and thought pattern of the depressed person. He remains stuck to his habits. He is lost in his own world. He sometimes becomes so depressed that he even stops talking to anyone . . . . and sometimes he becomes so lost that he commits suicide.

While staying at the hostel, I had started developing some serious neurological problems. It had created a number of issues in my life. I used to stand at the door for a long time staring the tap, shower, geyser switches and light switches.

The problem was that I could not make out whether the tap was closed or not, geyser switches were off or not and the light switches were on or not. When I used to check the tap, it first appeared clear, then it appeared hazy and then it used to become almost invisible to me. Sometimes, I used to stand at the door for fifteen minute. During those moments, I felt like killing myself. I was experiencing the same vision for everything. Sometimes, if I spot a person wearing spectacles which David wore, I used to start staring that spectacles and get completely lost into it. This would make that person annoyed. If it was a girl, she could not resist her laughter.

Either I would not be able to concentrate totally or I would concentrate too deeply costing the word 'concentration' look small for it. I could not even decide that the lock was closed or not. To confirm its state, I would pull the lock forcefully. Sometimes, while pulling it forcefully, I used to get hurt. Then, Katie would come running to give me first aid and then leave me as quickly as possible because she knew that I got angry on seeing her. Katie knew that she had become a hurdle between me and Carol and that I wanted Carol in my life at any cost.

I had no words in my dictionary to describe my love for Carol as well as my hatred for Katie. It's true that I broke the heart of someone who always stood beside me; whether I was bright in studies or a dullard . . . . actually I never wanted or intended to be a bright student. Katie herself came to my room every now and then because she knew that I would never go to her myself.

During her stay at New York, Carol used to go to a park near her hostel in the morning and in the evening, with her friends. I tried to meet her there but she ignored me at place too. Sometimes, I stood there for hours waiting for her in that park just hoping that someday she'll notice me.

Carol's love has blinded me to such an extent that I could not see Katie's love for me. I used to think that my life is of no use without Carol. Being obsessed with Carol's love, I did not even realise that a much better life could be possible for me of course it could be with Katie.

Carol had broken my heart many times, but there was a particular incident which was deeply imprinted on my mind . . . . and gave me a prolonged heartache. I was at an institute where a seminar was being conducted. Before the beginning of the seminar, students were sitting in the garden of that institute. They were waiting for the seminar to start. I was sitting on the blocks of stone which were cubical in shape. Those blocks were laid alongside the boundary of the garden.

Hardly fifteen minutes might have passed since I entered that institute, when a girl, dressed in a red sweatshirt(with black check lines on it) and blue cotton jeans, and a medium-sized shopping bag hung on her shoulder, breezed past me. She looked into my eyes for a fraction of a second leaving behind an uncertainty that whether she recognised me or not. Before

I could wish her with a smile or say anything to her, she passed by me making me feel that she didn't know me . . . . as if I wasn't even worthy of her time . . . . as if I was the person whom she hated the most . . . . as if I was inferior to her in some level. I was very much disheartened at that. I was feeling worthless inside of me. I didn't even look at her nor hoped that she would turn and look at me. For a moment, I was completely lost into myself. I didn't know what to do. I felt that I was good for nothing. I was feeling embarrassed though no one around me had done anything wrong to me. For a moment, I wanted to leave that institute and run back home but I didn't want to do this.

Strange thoughts started coming to my mind I realised that the chances of Carol to be my love were almost nil . . . . I also experienced big changes in me . . . . I felt my as if my attraction towards Carol was wearing down Carol stopped looking like a person for whom I would crave for.

I was so disappointed that even if Carol had come to hug me, I would not have felt anything. I felt as if I had lost my complete interest in Carol as well as from the love I once expected from her. I couldn't understand what had happened to me. Did I intentionally take back the love from myself? No. I think, it just got vanished by itself. It was hard to believe that such a small incident could change me so much. Was that incident worth that much? Certainly, that small act of her must have some greater meaning for me.

After the seminar ended, I decided to go home alone by myself but Katie's faithful guard was standing at the gate. His eyes got fixated just on my arrival. So, I had to go with him unwillingly.

When I reached home, that is Katie's house, the lunch was ready. I had that too unwillingly.

After eating the lunch, I came to my room, and till the night, I didn't come out. I knew that Carol could never be mine. Eventually, I have to slog with a person who will make me irritated with her love.

Throughout these years I struggled with the mental stress but it had peaked at that stage. I felt defeated . . . . so I decided to commit suicide. I wrote a suicide note. Apart from the other things, I also wrote that I have no complains or personal grudges against anyone, and that no one except me is solely responsible for my death.

I felt like breaking down in tears. I kept that suicide note inside my book and went to the washroom. There I saw reflection on a large mirror which covered almost half of the wall. I had never seem such a miserable image of myself. I could see the brightness and glow disappearing and leaving my face as dull and pale. Truly, I had never been so much soaked up into my sadness in my entire life.

My life seemed unbearable to me. I wept bitterly.

Tears were rolling down the cheeks.

Just then, Katie arrived home, though she was supposed to come a bit later. In other words, it was my luck because in her presence I couldn't dare to end my life.

As per her routine, she straightaway came to my room. I didn't know that she had entered.

When Katie didn't find me on the bed and on chair, she sat on the bed and opened my story book; co- incidentally, it was the same book in which I had kept the suicide note. Noticing the light from the little space below the door, she understood that I was in the washroom. When she was casually going through the book, she found that note. When she read it, she felt as if somebody pulled the rug from under her feet. She ran towards the washroom and started banging the door continuously.

"Open the door, Cyril! Open the door . . . .! Cyril, stay calm . . . . take it easy . . . . Cyril, we'll have a talk with Carol if you want . . . . we'll have a talk with her. I know, you are depressed but please . . . . please don't do such a terrible thing. I promise you, we'll have a talk with Carol if you want", her voice becoming more and more hesitating due to fear.

I was weeping uncontrollably. While weeping, I struggled hard to speak, "I . . . . I .... I don't want to talk to her I don't love her anymore". When this sentence finished, I wept like anything.

"Cyril, please, open the door. Everything will be alright . . . . Please open . . . . Please!", Katie's voice was more in control now than before.

I was already feeling very guilty for her. Soon, I opened the door slowly. I myself don't know the reason behind opening the door so slowly...... Maybe, I was not completely in my senses.

As I opened the door, Katie swiftly pulled me towards herself and closed the door. Then, she took me in her arms.

"What were you going to do?", Katie said. Tears began to roll down her cheeks.

I hugged her. I was also weeping. "I'm sorry . . . . I'm sorry . . . . I . . . . I love you . . . . I love you the most", I said while weeping. My 'sorry' was due to the guilt for hurting her so much and for trying to kill myself.

We had never come so close to each other. And, for Katie, it was beyond her expectations.

We sat on the chairs. Katie gave me a glass of water. "Did you read that note?", I asked.

"Yes, I did. I was going through your book. Actually, I wanted to put this chocolate in your book so that when you open it to read, you'll get a surprise", Katie replied. I told her that I had decided to commit suicide after coming out of the washroom.

Katie said, "I thought, you'd commit it in the washroom itself".

We had a long conversation, and we also sorted out our issues.

Few minute after that long conversation, Katie's brother came in. He had returned from the office. All three of us chatted a lot but neither Katie nor I let him know what a terrible thing was about to happen before he came.

Katie's parents had also accompanied her brother to home but they were on the ground floor. They were busy in their business discussions.

That day, I wanted to have my dinner with Katie only and that too in my room, but seeing the heartily will of Katie and her brother to eat together, I changed my mind.

We three went downstairs to join the parents at the dinner table, like we always did.

I came down thinking – "On one side, there's a girl, because of whose one small act, I was about to commit suicide, and on the other side, there's a girl, because of whose one small act, I changed my decision of committing suicide What a girl the latter one is!'.

Though I was feeling normal now, a little bit of aftershock of the incident was still there on my face. When Katie's parents asked me if I was alright, Katie, who had completely hid the aftershock effects of the incident from her face, defended me with her clever and witty answer.

After the dinner, Katie and I went off to my room. Katie sat beside me on the bed and I rested my head on her lap . . . . She was caressing her hand over my head . . . . sometimes she was touching and pulling my cheeks which I didn't like.

Now, everything was alright . . . . There was no one who was sad . . . . There was no one who was bickering about the precious life . . . . and . . . . There was . . . . nobody . . . . on the verge of suicide.

EPILOGUE

"I'm feeling too tired and sleepy", he said. It was evident from his eyes laden with fatigue. He needed some rest. He wanted to sit on the bed and then talk.

"Sir, please allow me to leave", I persuaded him and prepared myself to leave. "Sir, sorry to take your precious time . . . . Sir, I should go now", I said further. I knew he was not sleeping because of me. So I myself persuaded him.

He sat on the bed but asked me not to leave. I thought it was not right to act in such a manner on the very first day of my job. I was, actually, appointed as an assistant to the night warden.

"And there's one thing . . . . I was selected neither in Harvard nor in MIT . . . . In spite of getting that opportunity through Katie's help, I simply refused . . . . maybe because it would remind me of my pain . . . . but still, I'm very happy with my life . . . . I had no idea about such a joyful phase waiting for me on the other side of my life . . . . Now, Katie is my only love . . . . and Carol gone out of my list of loved ones forever . . . . I was right I was in fact wise enough to turn the sad page of my life's book",

he said in a very emotional tone.

He spoke no more . . . . He was looking pensive and emotional . . . . He was looking at the wall, completely lost in his own world.

There was a knock heard on the door. I opened the door and saw the warden standing a little away from it. He indicated me to come out.

"Sir, I should go now. Warden is calling me", I said politely. He smiled and said, "Okay!".

His humbleness had touched my heart.

The warden and I went to our room. We were talking to each other.

"He was once a resident of this hostel as a child and got too much attached to it", warden said.

"Yes, he told me about that", I replied.

"His wife, Katie, later bought this hostel from the owner, for him. She gave it to him as a surprise gift", warden said.

"What? I . . . . I didn't come to know about it . . . . he . . . . he didn't tell me about that. He didn't even let me feel about that. He was so down to earth", I replied in amazement.

The warden said, "Every week or so, he comes here with his wife, Katie, to spend at least two or three days. He takes that as a vacation".

"Where's Katie? Will she not come?", I asked.

The warden smiled. He replied, "Katie was in Room No. 4. She was sleeping. After you came out of the room, he went to Room No. 4 to wake her up. Then she moved to Room No. 5........ Didn't you come to know about that?", The warden smiled again.

I was totally in a surprised state.

Suddenly, the noise of opening of the hostel gates was heard. I saw a very large car strolling inside. It stood in the parking space.

A man, with a dress hung on a hanger, stepped out of the car.

"Who's he?", I asked the warden.

"He's Katie's brother. Katie had asked him to bring something that she had forgotten to bring with her. Actually, it was something related to Cyrus. Her brother had gone for that only", warden replied as he began to prepare for sleeping.

I saw Katie's brother. He was coming towards the inner entrance of the hostel . . . . Slowly the dress in his hand became clearly visible . . . . It was a pair of a sweatshirt and a trouser . . . . the trouser was . . . . dark black in colour . . . . and the sweatshirt dark brown.

*'Life is like a book. Turn its every page
rather than closing it in between'.*

Jack Stewart

Upcoming Novel

I HOPE

It's a story of a boy who dreams to explore the world. He is eager to know about the human feelings facing different situations in life. Every morning, he wakes up with some hope in his heart.